pocketbooks 04

The site of the new Scottish Parliament, Autumn 1999.
Photograph, Zoë Irvine © 2000.

Without Day

proposals for a new Scottish Parliament

Without Day

Edited by
Alec Finlay

With an Introduction by
David Hopkins

pocketbooks
Morning Star Publications
City Art Centre
Polygon

2000

Published by:
pocketbooks
Canongate Venture (5), New Street, Edinburgh EH8 8BH.

Morning Star Publications
Canongate Venture (5), New Street, Edinburgh EH8 8BH.

City Art Centre
2 Market Street, Edinburgh EH1 1DE.

Polygon
22 George Square, Edinburgh EH8 9LF.

Typeset in Minion and Univers.
Designed by Lucy Richards and Matthew Chapman, with Alec Finlay.
Printed and bound by Redwood Books Limited, Trowbridge.

Printed on Munken Elk 90gsm available from Trebruk UK Limited.

Published with the assistance of a grant from the Scottish Arts Council National
Lottery Fund and a grant from Highlands & Islands Enterprise (HI Arts).

A CIP record is available from the British Library.

ISBN 0 7486 6277 4

List of Contents

Dedicated to Hamish Henderson and George Elder Davie.

For a new Scottish Parliament

An upturned boat
   – a watershed

Kathleen Jamie

Editor's Acknowledgements

The original idea for this book arose out of an evening's conversation with Charles Esche, during which we plotted an exhibition surveying Conceptual art in Scotland at the Scottish National Gallery of Modern Art. This seemed then, and still does now, an unlikely prospect. We also discussed what art might feature in the new Parliament, and how a generation of young Scottish artists were unlikely to be considered.

At the time the siting and design of the Parliament had yet to be settled; now that it has, the idea of a 'drop' sculpture placed outside (or inside) the building Enric Miralles is creating seems a dreary and unnecessary convention. Having seen Miralles deliver two wonderful lectures, these *Without Day* proposals seem to me to be in sympathy with his ideas. If his buildings are, in his own words, a form of spatial 'writing', inscribed in architectural forms and shadows, then this book exists as an inventory of imaginings for that real and imaginary site.

The *Without Day* project is not a criticism of whatever works of art may at some future date be placed in or alongside the completed Parliament; rather it presents many possibilities, gathered together in a form which is modest enough to be held in the hand, yet is adventurous in the claims it makes on the readers' imagination.

The project reflects my practice as an artist and publisher, inviting contributions from others which are gathered into an anthology. I decided on the simplest possible form for the proposals: text, presented without image, to ensure the scale remained imaginative. The project stands alongside the work of a number of contemporary artists, poets and curators who have presented imaginary or unrealised projects, interventions or proposals; these include Ian Hamilton Finlay, John Latham, Nathan Coley (*Urban Sanctuary*), Tilo Schultz (*E.W.E.*), Douglas Gordon, Thomas A. Clark, Tom Leonard (*Situations Theoretical and Contemporary*), and Hans Ulrich Obrist (*Dreams*); comrades on a synchronous adventure into the non-material world.

There are many people to thank for help in realising this project; first and foremost, Jane Warrilow of the City Art Centre (Edinburgh), co-curator of the exhibition which accompanies this book. I would also like to thank the contributors for their forbearance in what has been a lengthy project, and to thank those contributors whose work could not be included because of space. The selectorial advisors for the project were Murdo Macdonald (University of Dundee), Ben Spencer, Andrew Patrizio (Edinburgh College of Art), and Jane Warrilow.

Murdo also provided the title, via George Elder Davie, which is such an apt summation, both in its reference to the Scottish philosophical tradition, and in describing proposals which will never be realised. The extract Murdo quotes in the letter which follows is from the long essay 'The Scottish Enlightenment' in Davie's *The Scottish Enlightenment and Other Essays*. Thanks are also due to Robert Crawford for permission to reprint 'Recall', and to Kathleen Jamie for the epigraph poem, from her latest collection, *Jizzen*.

I would like to thank Cluny Sheeler and Naomi West who worked on the typescript; Ken Cockburn and Alison Humphry of pocketbooks; Alison Bowden, Ian Davidson and Jeanie Scott of Polygon, and Andrew MacDougall of Scottish Book Source; Lucy Richards and Matthew Chapman, for the clarity of their design; Chad MacCail and Zoë Irvine, for creating the front cover and frontispiece respectively; Charles Esche, for his encouragement; and William Furlong for creating, with Aeolus and a number of volunteers, such a wonderful work of audio art for the first of the pocketbook CDs.

Finally, I would like to thank Zoë Irvine and Thomas Evans, for their comradeship and support during the realisation of *Without Day*.

29 November 1999

Alec Finlay
pocketbooks
Edinburgh

Dear Eck,

Here is the quote from George Davie that I mentioned to you – my first awareness of 'without day/sine die'.

. . . in order to keep their consciences right in the matter of first principles, they refused to vote their parliament out of existence at its final meeting, simply proroguing it sine die. They thus allowed the debate to continue on an intellectual plane, and enabled Francis Hutcheson to argue, in post-1730 Glasgow, that the Union was defective in failing to provide Scotland with institutional machinery for defending its rights as a nation.

This seems to sum up something of the metaphysical Scotland of which George has made sure we remain aware. (As we wait for the roses and geans to bloom.)

Best wishes

Murdo Macdonald

Without Day: Notes On Utopian Proposals
(With All Kinds Of Delays)

Existence, somebody said, is elsewhere . . .

And we all know the future never happens. Or rather never the way we planned it . . .

This publication envisages a real enough event; a long awaited symbolic moment. But its underlying theme, in many ways, is the unrealizable, the utopian, the chimerical even . . . With that in mind I shall begin by conjuring up a spiritual mentor for this collection of bittersweet proposals.

He is not particularly glamorous at first glance. Each day, for much of his life, he busies himself in the commercial district of Lyons working as a cloth merchant. Each morning, regular as clockwork, he takes his glass of wine at an unassuming café on the rue Saint-Marie-des-Terreaux. He returns alone each evening to his rented rooms. As far as we know he has never had a long lasting romantic attachment. But his unremarkable, slightly melancholy routines are the engine behind volumes of writing. Each night he continues his task, driven by two unshakeable convictions, 'absolute doubt' and 'absolute deviation' with regards to what passes as civilised life. Patiently, over the years, he constructs a universe built out of longings. Society will be governed by laws of 'passionate attraction', free love will become the social norm, work will be creative rather than repetitive and boring, people will live in what he calls 'Harmony' . . .

Such dreams sound familiar enough, not to say hackneyed. But he is one of the first to construct a full-scale project out of such imaginings, at least on behalf of the common man or woman. Let's get down to detail. 'Every passion that is suffocated', he says, with admirable introspection, 'produces a counter-passion, which is as malignant as the natural passion would have been benign.'[1] Long before Freud or Nietzsche or the Surrealists, then, he sees people as ruled by their psychological drives, their 'passions'. His mission is to conceive of a world that acknowledges and makes use of the perverse logic of the passions, rather than rationalising them away . . .

Slowly, paradoxically, he turns his libertarian dream into an exact science. A beautiful fanaticism enters into his ruminations. There are, he calculates, 810 common personality types, each corresponding to twelve basic passions. Doubling the figure to account for women as well as men, he arrives at the number 1620 which will constitute the optimal number for one of his 'Phalanxes' (the ideal communities or 'communes' in which members of a future society will live.) The structure of one of these 'Phalanxes' takes account of a range of ages from 0-100 and a finely-calibrated scale of personality types ranging from 'athletic' and 'virile' to 'refined' and 'temperate'.

The detail becomes increasingly labyrinthine and idiosyncratic. In accordance with the idea that differing personality types naturally gravitate towards divergent activities, he creates work programmes or 'passionate series' in which the permutations of even the most rudimentary tasks conform to the personalities of the workers. Particularly drawn to pears among the agricultural produce of the Phalanxes, he considerately matches people to pear types, although here a militaristic logic clearly creeps into the schema concerned:

	Pear Growers Series	
Divisions	Progression	Types
Forward outpost	2 groups	Quinces and abnormally hard types
Ascending wingtip	4 groups	Hard Cooking Pears
Ascending wing	6 groups	Crisp Pears
Centre of the series	8 groups	Juicy Pears
Descending wing	6 groups	Compact pears
Descending wingtip	4 groups	Mealy pears
Rear outpost	2 groups	Medlars and abnormally soft types[2]

Further refinements are built into the overall model; workers of a 'Butterfly' type 'flutter from pleasure to pleasure'. They will therefore be allowed to move between occupations, sampling as many as eight tasks in various 'work series' during the course of a day. On the other hand, there is a 'Cabalist' element in many workers, a tendency towards tribalism. Such instincts can be harnessed to ensure a healthy degree of rivalry between workers' groups, but the influence of the 'Cabalists' will nevertheless be moderated via the infiltration of the 'Butterfly' types . . .

Work will also be attuned to age. He solves the problem of recruiting people for menial tasks, or as he says 'work devoid of attraction' with a master stroke. Close attention to the psychology of children yields the following:

> *Two thirds of all boys have a penchant for filth. They love to wallow in the mire and play with dirty things. They are unruly, peevish, scurrilous and overbearing . . . These children will enroll in the Little Hordes whose task it is to perform, dauntlessly and as a point of honour, all those loathsome tasks that ordinary workers would find debasing . . . they will be divided into three corps: the first is assigned to foul functions such as sewer cleaning, tending the dung heap, working in the slaughter-houses etc . . .* [3]

I should step back here and provide some form of context. Our man is Charles Fourier, the early nineteenth century French 'utopian socialist'. His ideas were to find a muffled echo in later socialist schemes; Marx and Engels in *The German Ideology* flirted momentarily with the possibility that, under socialism, the worker would be able to 'hunt in the morning, fish in the afternoon, rear cattle in the evening, engage in criticism after dinner.' [4] But Fourier's genius resides in the poetry that emanates from his weird collisions of psychology and systematism and the magnificent impracticality of his proposals. In this he resembles those quirky late eighteenth-century French Neo-classical architects, Boulée and Ledoux. The latter's 'Design for a House' of 1790 envisages enormous futuristic looking spheres nestling improbably in a park setting. (Eighteenth-century martians might at any moment emerge from their tiny doorways and parade down the elaborate stairways.)

It is not surprising that it was André Breton, the 'pope' of Surrealism, who helped rehabilitate Fourier's reputation this century, writing an 'Ode to Charles Fourier' in 1945. The clearest annexation of Fourier to twentieth-century sensibility is effected, however, by Roland Barthes, who inserts our dreamer into the company of a sadist and a saint in *Sade/Fourier/Loyal* (1971). Barthes shrewdly writes: 'Fourier is like a child . . . discovering with enchantment the exorbitant power of combinatory analysis or geometrical progression. In the end, the number itself is not needed for this exaltation; we need only subdivide a class in order triumphantly to achieve this paradox: a detail (literally minutia) magnifies, like joy. It is a fury of expansion, of possession, and, in a word, of orgasm, by number, by classification: scarcely does an object appear than Fourier taxonomizes.'[5]

With Barthes it is the eccentric structural equivalences within Fourier's 'closed system' that call out to us. Bourgeois-liberal morality, and the trajectories of rational thought undergirding it, gradually lose their grip as Fourier tabulates the Byzantine details of the orgies in store for his Phalanx dwellers. A poetics, or erotics, of megolamania takes hold. The totalizing power of the imaginary turns totalitarian. As Fourier's imaginings extend geographically or rather globally, they become increasingly exorbitant. Since the rules of 'passionate attraction' extend to the heavenly bodies, he asserts that the earth itself will change in accordance with new cosmic rhythms. Grapes will grow in St Petersburg and the northern seas will apparently turn into a 'sort of lemonade'. Ultimately, and disturbingly, we get an uncanny premonition of the recorded 'table-talk' of a rather different utopian, Adolf Hitler, who, similarly fastening onto Russia as the site of his wilder speculations, estimated that the German conquerors of the Ukraine would 'build spaghetti factories on the spot; all the prerequisites are there . . .'[6]

This fleeting kinship between Fourier and Hitler might indicate that we should look for inspiration to more sober 'utopian socialists'. What about the Factory reformer Robert Owen, who set up cotton mills at New Lanark in Scotland in 1799, ran them in accordance with unheard-of principles of 'human perfectibility' and eventually dreamt of a 'new moral world' consisting of co-operative villages in which private property was abolished? Or Saint Simon in France, who echoed Owen in foreseeing that it would be under an industrial dispensation that the common man's meagre glimpse of freedom would be envisaged? But in the end such visions are simply accommodations to the status quo. And aren't they just a little bit dour? Isn't the spirit of this *Without Day* project a positive affirmation of impossibility? (And isn't there a certain order of politics lodged in that recognition?).

* * *

Many of the short proposals that follow implicitly acknowledge the impossibility of their realisation. However, perhaps not all of the writers would subscribe to my promotion of Fourier, however beguiling his insanities. For a generation of artists and writers who grew up, or were born, in the wake of 1968, Fourier no doubt seems far too unironic, too much the prototype Surrealist or hippy. Ultimately the forms of a post-Duchampian conceptualism underpin the *Without Day* project; and Duchamp's own fragmentary proposals studiously assume a dystopian tenor: 'Establish a society/in which the individual/has to pay for the air he breathes/air metres . . . in the case of non-payment/simple asphyxiation if/necessary (cut off the air).[7] Even more appropriately Duchamp's practice was imbued with the politics of impossibility. Delay was a fundamental principle in his universe; delay built into the very conditions for thoughts, actions and projects as if to concede in advance that they would be 'without day'. Ruminating on a strategy for designating one of his 'readymades' (objects not made by the artist but *chosen* as works of art) he notes: 'Specifications for "Readymades". By planning for a moment to come (on such a day, such a date, such a minute), "to inscribe a readymade" – the readymade can be later looked for (with all kinds of delays.)'[8]

Conceptualists from the late 1960s onwards inherited something of their dry, parodically bureaucratic tone from Duchamp. Their propositions, however tersely worded, nevertheless exhibited a magnanimous openness with regards to their potential (if possible) realisation. Among the proposals of one early exponent of Conceptual art, Lawrence Weiner, we find multiple instances where the possibility of physical realisation dissolves, as it were, into the fabric of language or thought:

An amount of bleach poured upon a rug and allowed to bleach (1968)

One standard Air Force dye marker thrown into the sea (1968)

Two other early Conceptualists, Terry Atkinson and Mike Baldwin, later to be part of the Art & Language collective, put on an 'Air Show/Air-Conditioning Show' in Coventry in 1966-7. The show consisted of a proposal for a: ' "column" of air, atmosphere, "void" etc' – although the artists were at pains to point out that: 'none of this is to say that a complete, if only "factual" or constructual, specification is to be expected.'[9] Whether utopianism of any kind is strictly at issue here is doubtful. Although the heady moment of 1968 was just around the corner it might have seemed that only the pure possibility of the impossible (or vice versa) legitimately stood to be addressed . . .

The continuing life of the unrealised or unrealizable proposal is in the hands of writers such as those featured in this anthology. Yet their texts, like those of their utopian forebears, rarely smack of the professional writers' métier. Contributions by artists, architects, poets, performers, dreamers – some ironic, some 'innocent' in tone – are gathered side by side. Often they harbour a little (veiled) utopianism. Leaving them to speak for themselves, I leave the final word to one of the progenitors of a more satirical form of social imagining. Like Fourier, some of Jonathan Swift's finest (albeit darkest) moments came when devising schemes that made use of children. In *A Modest Proposal*, written in 1729 as a blueprint for ridding Ireland of the drain on its resources represented by the children of the poor, he wrote:

> *I do therefore humbly offer it to public consideration that of the hundred and twenty thousand children already computed, twenty thousand may be reserved for breed . . . (whilst) the remaining hundred thousand may, at a year old, be offered in sale to the persons of quality and fortune through the kingdom; always advising the mother to let them suck plentifully in the last month, so as to render them plump and fat for the table. A child will make two dishes at an entertainment for friends; and when the family dines alone, the fore or hind quarters will make a reasonable dish.*[10]

Swift was careful to enumerate the social advantages of his plan. Conscious of Ireland's obligations to England, he noted: 'we can incur no danger in disobliging England. For the commodity will not bear exportation, the flesh being of too tender a consistence to admit a long continuance in salt.'[11] His ear for the hypocrisies and self-deluding homilies that fuel much public discourse was unerring. Let us hope that a future parliament registers both the spirit of his proposal and of those that follow.

David Hopkins teaches in the School of Art History at the University of St Andrews. His co-authored book *Marcel Duchamp* is part of Thames and Hudson's World of Art series and his study of late twentieth century art, *After Modern Art: 1945-2000* appears as part of Oxford University Press's Oxford History of Art series in September 2000. He also writes and performs poetry.

Notes

1   Quoted in J. Beecher and R. Bienvenu (eds), The Utopian Vision of Charles Fourier, London, 1975, p.41
2   Ibid p.47
3   Fourier 'Work Problems in Harmony', as quoted in Beecher and Bienvenu, Utopian Vision, p.317
4   Quoted Beecher and Bienvenu, ibid p.70
5   Barthes, Sade/Fourier/Loyola, trans. R. Miller, London, 1976, p.104
6   Hitler's Table-Talk 1941-44 (trans. Cameron and Stevens, London, 1953) cited in John Carey (ed), The Faber Book of Utopias, London, 1999, p.425
7   Marcel Duchamp, The Bride Stripped Bare by her Bachelors, Even (The Green Box Notes), New York, 1960, unpaginated
8   Ibid
9   Quoted in Lucy Lippard, Six Years: The Dematerialisation of the Art Object, reprinted University of California Press, 1997, p.21
10   Swift, A Modest Proposal, reprinted Cologne, 1997, p.207
11   Ibid, p.213

Recall

I have recalled the Scottish Parliament
From hatbands and inlaid drawers,

From glazed insides of earthenware teapots,
Corners of greenhouses, tumblers

Where it has lain in session too long,
Not defunct but slurring its speeches

In a bleary, irresolute tirade
Affronting the dignity of the house,

Or else exiled to public transport
For late-night sittings, the trauchled members

Slumped in wee rows either side of the chamber
Girning on home through the rain.

My aunt died, waiting for this recall
In her Balfron cottage. I want her portrait

Hung with those of thousands of others
Who whistled the auld sang toothily under their breath.

Let her be painted full-length, upright
In her anorak, flourishing secateurs.

She knew the MPs in funny wigs
Would return bareheaded after their long recess

To relearn and slowly unlearn themselves,
Walking as if in boyhood and girlhood

They'd just nipped down to the shops for the messages
And taken the winding path back.

Robert Crawford

Without Day proposals for a new Scottish Parliament

A Proposal for a Book: *Without Day*

An invitation, circulated as widely as possible, seeking written proposals for a new Scottish Parliament. These proposals may take the form of an event, work of art, or some other kind of intervention, in any media. They may be intended for the new Parliament building which is being designed by Enric Miralles, or for the occasion of a new Scottish Parliament in the widest sense. None of the proposals will be realised. They are in this sense 'without day'. Freed from physical or temporal limitations they may be monumental, or suggest the smallest intervention, action, or idea without physical form.

The final selection was made by a panel comprising Murdo MacDonald (University of Dundee), Ben Spencer, Andrew Patrizio (Edinburgh College of Art) and Jane Warrilow (City Art Centre). Published by pocketbooks; copublished by Polygon, Morning Star Publications and City Art Centre (Edinburgh); *Without Day* accompanies an exhibition of the same name at the City Art Centre, April 8th-June 3rd 2000.

Alec Finlay

A Proposal for a special edition of *Without Day*

A special edition of *Without Day* will be published, consisting of as many copies as there were days between the suspension of the sitting of the last Scottish Parliament on 28th April 1707, until the recall of Parliament on May 6th 1999.

This edition will be available free from the foyer of the new Parliament (and nowhere else). The gradual distribution of the books throughout Scotland and abroad will echo the flow of the democratic process from the Parliament building to the wider world.

A Proposal for Without Day

The site for the new Scottish Parliament should be levelled.

The periphery of the site should then be planted with mature birch, larch and pine. This must be as dense as possible. The inner area should be planted with the same species but more randomly and far less dense.

On completion the new Parliament should then be able to go about its business.

Graham Fagen

A Proposal: Generation Room

I would like to propose that a space be identified within the new building and be named the Generation Room. An interior space, the manufacture of which begins on the opening day of the new Parliament.

A room designed and constructed using the most expensive and rare materials and employing craftsmen and women from around the world. Mixing the modern with the ancient, the new and the old and the radical with the traditional. The design should produce an environment of such significance as to be discussed by all of Scotland. A room which when visited will create adoration, wonder and disbelief in the eyes of visitors.

The timescale for its completed construction should be placed at 35 years, the period of a generation.

Nathan Coley

A Proposal: The Cairn of Commitment

Six local stones of a portable weight are smoothed by artists and inscribed with Celtic curves and a motto of no more than six words of commitment by local MSPs, who pay for this work to be done. The stones are left beside flowing or standing water in each constituency, although not too dangerously placed. People who find the stones are entitled to travel free to Edinburgh to place their stone on a cairn in the Parliament grounds, around which water flows. The words on each stone are inscribed on a polished granite block nearby, with the names of the finders and the date of each commitment's discovery. Every six years, the stones are used in a ceremonial curling match involving teams of citizens and politicians at Hogmanay, and the Cairn of Commitment is then rebuilt.

James McGonigal

A Proposal: The Wayside Orators Platform

A speakers' corner is to be established near to the entrance of the new Parliament building; a place where the unofficial, impromptu, radical or dissenting voice may be heard, within earshot of the home of the official national representatives.

A traditional wooden soap box is to be cast in bronze and situated within a paved area. It is envisaged that orators will use this platform to discuss matters of local and national importance. Sufficient space should be provided around the box for a small crowd to gather.

An inscription (taken from Plato, *The Laws*, Book VI) on the box will read:

> *our scheme is only a sketch*

A Proposal for Without Day

May a circle of twenty-eight rowan trees be planted around the new Parliament building.

Every year when the trees are heavy with fruit and ready to yield, some of the fruit should be taken, leaving a fair portion for the birds and other animals.

A jelly should be made with the fruit, to be served to all the members of parliament and all who work there. May they be reminded of the trees and the animals in the wild places that they also represent and remember to protect them.

Jayne Wilding

A Proposal: Opening

That every window of the Parliament building be blocked out with a paste of lard and bird seed, obscuring all daylight inside. These to be covered in turn with a temporary shuttering and at a given time all shutterings to be removed. The Parliament is open when the birds have finished, the last window is completely clear and daylight enters freely.

Marion Coutts

A Proposal: The Line

A line will be cast in bronze.

The line will be 16cm deep, 2cm wide.

The length will be dictated by the width of the main entrance of the building as it will fit comfortably within that entrance.

The line will be inserted into the floor of the entrance to sit flush with the ground. The line will be installed along the threshold of the building – along the margin where interior and exterior space meet.

The line will take its form as a scaled down version of that greater line where the peninsulas of Scotland and England meet – commonly referred to as 'the border'.

When installed it will not be possible to enter the Parliament building without crossing the line.

Despite the actual alignment of the entrance of the building, the line will serve as a reminder to those entering the building that they are stepping North-westwards over a line that defines the beginning of Scottish space.

Donald Urquhart

Balance. Poise. The gentle pirouette of Janus on the door step, his moment
before invocation, convocation. Not indecision but that flexing hesitation
where thought gathers and matures before words marshal sense into
fruitful law. Hail to the thresholds of a Scottish Parliament! Neither of
chambers, ante-rooms or corridors. Nor without them. But slight borders,
unnoticed margins, hems to the ermine, light-filled spaces of debate. No
thresholds barred! No threshold; yet present everywhere, anytime; shape
of shadow cast through window, stone's lip of cement and mortar, the
frame of someone's glasses glinting reminding you of frailty and vision.
Threshold is amendment. Modest footnote on the door-stane, drumming
of fingers on tables where just forms of words are sought. In Scots it's
threshwart, thrashel, lintel and doorsole. And in the door's soul the days
with all their differences and contradictions are visible. And they are held
in the palm of door-sole and communicate, commune with all within
doors that is common, the same as we seem we've always been, folk from
this airt. The thresholds of a Scottish Parliament are palms that sign its
body with the timbre of heel and instep, discreet life-line, pinkie and little
toe. They sign the etymology of 'threshold', our foreign roots reminding
us that once here was there, that once all of us were them, saying, signing
do not slam the door on threscwald, threxwold; from thresc-an ferire, and
wald liguum, i.e. the wood which one strikes with one's feet at entering or
going out of a house. Do not slam the door on South Germany's trooskel,
Denmark's taerskel or Iceland's throskulld-ur. Within the door-stane
smeddum of the thresholds of a Scottish Parliament the delicate hyphens
pivot, rocking its people inwards, outwards to the translated melodies of
Alexander Carmichael's blessing:

Grace of the threshold be thine
Grace of floor and ceiling
From site to stay
From beam to wall,
From balk to roof-tree,
From found to summit
    Found and summit

Here is the morning-evening blessing of the house, the Gaelic-Scots-English, each inflecting each, each turned to each. Strike hard upon this wood. Knock upon the wood of the great boat shapes an architect has placed above our heads in echo of the sailing thresholds of our Parliament.

David Kinloch

A Proposal: You Mark My Words

This project celebrates the Calvinist Grandmother, at once a Scottish archetype deeply etched in our collective psyche and a real woman, scourge of the Life-Force everywhere. I propose a series of epigrams, prominently inscribed into the stonework surrounding the entrance to our Parliament:

If ye look intae thon mirror ony mair, yell see The Devil

Yer smiling noo but yell soon be laughin on the other side o yer fais

Yer faither/mither/brither/sister wiz just as bad

What's comin fur ye will no go past ye

If ye dinnae wipe that smirk aff yer fais
yell be hanged as a murderer wan day

YOU MARK MY WORDS

Such instances of philosophical brilliance should engender an appropriate sense of humility all too lacking, alas, among the class of citizens liable to enter the sphere of political endeavour and subsequent advancement. These worthy sentiments should act as a counterbalance against vanity and hubris and will be witnessed daily by the humbled MSP as he or she approaches the Holyrood Parliament. Our elected representative will enter the Chamber suitably chastened and guilt-ridden, ears ringing with the invocations of The Calvinist Granny.

Bill Duncan

A Proposal for Two Piles of Plaques for the Scottish Parliament Building

Two piles of paper, immaculately, indeed magically lain, one on the next, so as to make the appearance of a single column of fine, nay, filo layers, slivers of marble. These are to be placed on either side of the grand entrance (should there be a grand entrance) of the new building. As this is to be 'Without Day', I can categorically state it will also be without wind, thus the piles will remain unmoved by accident of god.

One of the piles will comprise paper, printed with the following quote from Plato, *The Republic* (Book VII, Part VII):

And so our state and yours will be really awake, and not merely dreaming like most societies, with their shadow battles and their struggles for political power, which they treat as some great prize.

The second of the piles will be made up of paper, printed with the quote above, but altered using the simple procedure of NV+7 (i.e. the nouns and verbs 'moved on' by seven definitions in a dictionary), thus, from Platypus, *The Reredorter* (Moved on VII):

And so our statesmen and yours will be really awkward, and not really dribbling like most sockets, with their shag battlers and their struttings for political pox, which they tremble as some great probe.

The people may take one sheet from either pile, taking the utmost care so as not to disturb the ordered structure. They may do with it as they please, though aeroplanes and bookmarks are recommended.

Gavin Jones

A Proposal:
One$_1$ to$_2$ twelve$_3$. The$_1$ new$_2$ parliament$_3$. A$_1$ glass-encapsulated$_2$ groundfloor$_3$.

Enter$_1$ through$_2$ three$_3$ perpetually$_4$ revolving$_5$ doors$_6$. There$_1$ is$_2$ an$_3$ open$_4$ plan$_5$ lobby$_6$. Several$_1$ columns$_2$ (human$_3$ high$_4$) move$_5$ freely$_6$. Four$_1$ paternosters$_2$ mark$_3$ an$_4$ internal$_5$ field$_6$. At$_1$ three$_2$ sides$_3$ long$_4$ low$_5$ tables$_6$. Then$_1$, seating$_2$, forms$_3$ of$_4$ decoration$_5$, flexibility$_6$.

The$_1$ columns$_2$: people$_3$ can$_4$ sever$_5$ pieces$_6$ from$_7$ their$_8$ trunks$_9$. The$_1$ material$_2$ properties$_3$ of$_4$ the$_5$ columns$_6$ are$_7$ not$_8$ fixed$_9$. They$_1$ can$_2$ change$_3$ according$_4$ to$_5$ individual$_6$ predilections$_7$ and$_8$ desires$_9$. They$_1$ may$_2$ be$_3$ soft$_4$, hard$_5$, talkative$_6$, sexy$_7$, large$_8$, etc$_9$. Each$_1$ severed$_2$ piece$_3$ may$_4$ hence$_5$ serve$_6$ a$_7$ different$_8$ function$_9$. Here$_1$ as$_2$ a$_3$ cushion$_4$, there$_5$ as$_6$ an$_7$ oratorial$_8$ device$_9$. It$_1$ will$_2$ become$_3$ one's$_4$ companion$_5$ piece$_6$ for$_7$ a$_8$ day$_9$. All$_1$ items$_2$ will$_3$ be$_4$ returned$_5$ at$_6$ the$_7$ day's$_8$ end$_9$. Despite$_1$ their$_2$ abundance$_3$, the$_4$ columns$_5$ don't$_6$ crowd$_7$ the$_8$ lobby$_9$.

The$_1$ free$_2$ standing$_3$ paternosters$_4$ limit$_5$ the$_6$ columns'$_7$ mobility$_8$ within$_9$ the$_{10}$ lobby$_{11}$ parameters$_{12}$. The$_1$ paternosters$_2$ themselves$_3$ move$_4$ the$_5$ parliamentarians$_6$ (or$_7$ any$_8$ visitor$_9$) to$_{10}$ the$_{11}$ assembly$_{12}$. Open$_1$ on$_2$ all$_3$ sides$_4$ they$_5$ appear$_6$ as$_7$ if$_8$ people$_9$ may$_{10}$ fall$_{11}$ off$_{12}$. Yet$_1$ from$_2$ the$_3$ interior$_4$ their$_5$ walls$_6$ are$_7$ glazed$_8$ with$_9$ a$_{10}$ shady$_{11}$ haze$_{12}$. On$_1$ each$_2$ landing$_3$ the$_4$ glazing$_5$ opens$_6$ for$_7$ people$_8$ to$_9$ step$_{10}$ out$_{11}$ safely$_{12}$. The$_1$ size$_2$ of$_3$ each$_4$ compartment$_5$ matches$_6$ the$_7$ size$_8$ of$_9$ the$_{10}$ revolving$_{11}$ doors$_{12}$. Their$_1$ three$_2$ dimensional$_3$ cross$_4$ shapes$_5$ spin$_6$ and$_7$ ascend$_8$/descend$_9$ at$_{10}$ regular$_{11}$ pace$_{12}$. With$_1$ synchronised$_2$ and$_3$ comparatively$_4$ static$_5$ movements$_6$ they$_7$ contrast$_8$ with$_9$ the$_{10}$ columns'$_{11}$ irregularity$_{12}$. The$_1$ spectacle$_2$ can$_3$ be$_4$ viewed$_5$ from$_6$ all$_7$ sides$_8$ – provided$_9$ there$_{10}$ is$_{11}$ light$_{12}$. Special$_1$ seating$_2$ and$_3$ low$_4$ tables$_5$ cater$_6$ for$_7$ comfortable$_8$ relaxation$_9$ amidst$_{10}$ flexible$_{11}$ decoration$_{12}$. Stem-like$_1$ structures$_2$ are$_3$ within$_4$ reach$_5$ which$_6$ can$_7$ be$_8$ adorned$_9$ with$_{10}$ anything$_{11}$ desirable$_{12}$. Pieces$_1$ from$_2$ the$_3$ columns$_4$ are$_5$ one$_6$ option$_7$ here$_8$ (erasers$_9$ or$_{10}$ petals$_{11}$, others$_{12}$?)

The$_1$ entrance$_2$ is$_3$ a$_4$ constantly$_5$ moving$_6$ situation$_7$. Yet$_1$ permanently$_2$ sited$_3$ – immobile$_4$. Both$_1$ functional$_2$ and$_3$ solely$_4$ aesthetic$_5$, providing$_6$ a$_7$ place$_8$ for$_9$ social$_{10}$ interaction$_{11}$. A$_1$ foundation$_2$ for$_3$ future$_4$ history$_5$. And$_1$ then$_2$? Each$_1$ day$_2$ will$_3$ project$_4$ a$_5$ new$_6$ visual$_7$ tactility$_8$. The$_1$ mechanics$_2$ will$_3$ remain$_4$ the$_5$ same$_6$ – the$_7$ design$_8$ may$_9$ change$_{10}$. History$_1$.

Jorn Ebner

A Proposal for Water Music Both Sides of the Tweed

A recording of the sounds of the flowing waters of all the burns, streams, becks and rivers that run along or intersect the Scotland/England border, sampled from their source in the Border hills, their confluences with other rivers, and at the point where they enter the sea. This water music can be heard sounding constantly but quietly around the perimeters of the new Parliament building.

Davy Polmadie

Air/Mind Disc

to be inscribed on the air of the central debating chamber of the
Scottish Parliament & traced on the memories of all who enter

hindrance, prevention, preclusion, obstruction, stoppage, interruption, interception,
creed, system of opinions, school, doctrine, articles, canons, tenets, credenda,
interclusion, impedition, retardment, retardation, embarrassment, oppilation, coarctation,
class, division, category, *categorema*, head, order, section, department,
stricture, restriction, restraint, inhibition, blockade, interference, interposition,
province, domain, kind, sort, genus, species, variety, family, race, tribe,
obtrusion, discouragement, discountenance, impediment, let, obstruction, knot,
caste, sept, clan, breed, type, kit, sect, set, assortment, feather, kidney,
knag, check, hitch, *contretemps*, screw loose, grit in the oil, bar, stile, barrier, turnstile,
suit, range, gender, sex, kin, manner, description, denomination,
turnpike, gate, portcullis, barricade, wall, dead wall, breakwater, groyne, bulkhead,
designation, aspect, phase, *phasis*, seeming, shape, guise, look,
block, buffer, stopper, boom, dam, weir, burrock, drawback, objection, stumbling-
complexion, colour, image, mien, air, cast, carriage, port, demeanour,
block, stumbling-stone, lion in the path, snag, snags and sawyers, encumbrance,
presence, expression, consanguinity, relationship, kindred, blood,

outwith
without

incumbrance, clog, skid, shoe, spoke, drag-chain, drag-weight, stay, stop, preventive,
parentage, filiation, affiliation, lineage, agnation, connection, next-of-kin,
prophylactic, load, burden, burthen, fardel, *onus*, millstone round the neck, *impedimenta*,
uncle, aunt, nephew, niece, cousin, first cousin, second cousin, cousin
dead weight, lumber, pack, nightmare, Ephialtes, incubus, old man of the sea, remora,
once removed, cousin twice removed, near cousin, distant cousin, relation,
difficulty, obstacle, estoppel, ill wind, head wind, trammel, tether, hold back,
brother, sister, fraternity, sorority, stock, *stirps*, side, strain, paternity,
counterpoise, damper, wet blanket, hinderer, marplot, killjoy, interloper,
parent, father, sire, dad, papa, *paterfamilias*, abba, genitor, progenitor,
trail of a red herring, opponent, **vow to help all beings without number**, thus: **ailm**,
procreator, ancestor, grandsire, grandfather, house, stem, trunk, tree,
beith, coll, darach, eadha, fearn, gort, uath, iogh, inis, muin, nuin, onn, ruis, siul, elm,
pedigree, line, forefathers, birth, ancestry, forebears, patriarchs,
birch, hazel, oak, aspen, alder, ivy, hawthorn, yew, blackthorn, vine, ash, whin, elder, sally,
motherhood, maternity, mother, dam, mama, *materfamilias*, grandmother, day

Gerry Loose

45

A Proposal: How to Springclean a New Scottish Parliament

1. On the first clear blue skies day in spring select as many naughty children from the local street corners as possible.

2. Bribe them into the main debating chamber of a new Scottish Parliament with a paper bag full of choice sweeties.

3. When the space is crammed full suggest that if they wish to blow into their empty paper bags and explode them together after three then this would be O.K.

Luci Ransome

Without Day

In Scotland's parliament I'd like to see
the corridors of power awash
with glacial slush
descended from the heights
of gleaming Sirius.

A transcendental landscape would emerge
like interstellar dream-space
dark immense
where every lesser star
could post its transience.

Entranced and learned seers would trace out
patterns in our moving chaos,
interpreters
who would translate for us
graceful calligraphies.

Scotland's parliament would be composed
from drops and lines of lyric wisdom
from epic poems
as memorably by heart
we'd make our turn our part.

Tessa Ransford

A Proposal for a banner hung above the speakers chair in the Debating
Chamber of the New Scottish Parliament
Counter-argument: Yes we can.

Sandy Salmon

A Proposal

It is proposed that the names of all the Munros be painted in grey Roman capitals onto the walls of the debating chamber of the new Scottish Parliament, as a reminder that the mountains have a vote.

Thomas A. Clark

A Proposal

A jam jar of wild flowers to be placed beside each member of the Scottish Parliament.

Winter

Yarrow
White Dead-nettle
Herb Robert
Old Man's Beard
Wood Spurge
Shepherd's Purse

Spring

Cuckoo flower
Coltsfoot
Primrose
Dog's Mercury
Ground Ivy
Speedwell

Summer

Meadow Cranesbill
Sainfoin
Ox-eye Daisy
Heartsease
Stitchwort
Lady's Bedstraw

Autumn

Harebell
Field Scabious
Red Clover
Chicory
Rosebay Willowherb
Eyebright

Laurie Clark

A Proposal: Scottish Thistle/English Rose

To reproduce the cornice (of English Roses and Scottish Thistles) presently decorating the ceiling of two adjoining rooms (East and West) of 15 Scotland Street Edinburgh (formerly Graeme Murray Gallery) and install it above the threshold of the Debating Chamber of the new Scottish Parliament.

Jim Hamlyn

A Proposal for an Open Kitchen

Situated in a central location within the new Scottish Parliament building would be a large open kitchen and dining area. The dining area would contain sufficient seating to accommodate all MSPs.

Each day a cross-party coalition of five members would prepare a lunch-time meal for their parliamentary colleagues. In the course of each year MSPs would be required to work in the kitchen on at least one occasion.

A Watermark for Scottish Education Department Stationery

idealsareinseparablefromaspirations

Kevin Henderson

A Bookshop for a New Scottish Parliament

Categories in order of yardage, greatest first:

1. Coffee Shop (no bookshop would be complete . . .).

2. Language section. Reflecting the 189 extant, 30 extinct and 18 million private languages which have a legitimate claim to be recognised as official in Scotland.

3. Fountain with breeding pair of Red Throated Divers.

4. Lost Worlds section. Hints on opium eating, body snatching and other savoury habits. Features Danish, Welsh/Brythonic, Jutish, GrecoRoman/ Italian and other Scottish cultures, now sadly removed or defunct.

5. Politics Section. Six books: *20,000 Leagues under the Sea, Life: A User's Manual, Pierrot Mon Ami, Hopscotch, Mr. Palomar, Birds of Britain and Europe* (Collins).

6. Geography Section. Two books: *How to Start Your Own Country,* by Erwin S. Strauss; and *The Observer's Book 11 (Aircraft)*, bought at a car boot sale in 1997 for 50p, signed on the first page S. V. Oliver Rafur(t) 1969.

7. Travel Section. Guides to Nova Scotia, Scotch Corner, Scotia Ridge, Scotia Sea, Scotland (Canada), Scotty's Junction, Scottburgh and Glasgow.

The layout of the Bookshop is to be as follows:

Shelving to be made of pure crystal glass, in a room (made of the same material) to be a perfect cube, 8m or yards (as is your wont) cubed. The sales desk is to be a single block of the crystal used above. It will be 1.35m cubed and must have NO bubbles, scratches or other blemishes on it.

The bookshop is to be positioned partly submerged in a cuboid lake (25m x 25m x 0.35m, or yards), of the purest spring water in a raised tank made of the above glass. The water must at all times be absolutely still.

Total silence within the shop and in the environs of the shop must be observed at all times, even when closed.

No element may be introduced into the shop which could: (a) break the silence, (b) break the glass, (c) break the surface of the water, or (d) break the sight lines.

Gavin Jones

A Proposal: Scottish Aeon

Qualifications for standing for election for a seat in the New Scottish
Parliament.

Grief and patience.

Having waited and endured
the best men and women
sail from Scottish harbours
hacking their way into remote blood.

Grief and patience.

Parliament will sit only on those days,
at those times
when the ghost of a teenage girl
drowned within sight
of the rocks of Nova Scotia

Brushes the building with her shawl;

The rest of the time Parliament
will be gone again, back under, dispersed
into the working hands of farms and warehouses,
shops and factories, streets and desks
of the Scottish people.

Grief and patience.

She will walk
to the stacked materials of the unstarted building
brushing bricks and insulation foam,
steel rods and concrete mixers with her shawl.

Once every hundred years.

During that time, for that time only,
builders with leather tool-belts,
hard, ribbed hats, northern food-boxes wild
with a hunger to get the building up
will start a trench, then pause
for a long season's ploughing,
schooling, burying their shocked dead.

When the building is built,
when there have been a hundred years of peace,
she will take the shawl from her back
and pass it to a living daughter
who will stroke, once, below the steps,
calming the phantoms in Scotland's gutter.

During that time, and that time only,
elected members
will attend to their building,
open their ordered papers,
and meet.

David Greenslade

A Proposal

Within the Scottish Parliament there will be 129 seats. There will be 73 Constituency Members. There will be 7 regional members from each of the 8 regions.[†] What of *without ?* 73 seats (city benches) arranged around a 219m ring define a common ground. Outer Diameter 71m (a radius of 35.5m). Inner diameter 70m (a radius of 35m). 3960m^2 in total would represent Scotland's land area. Each bench 2400 by 450mm in area, 1.085m.[††] The area covered by benches will be approximately 2% of the total 71m ring. Equal in proportion is the 2% of urban land area across Scotland, 98% rural land. A 10.89m square plinth of stone within the circle would represent 3% of rocky ground and mountain tops. Perhaps only 300mm high. Not necessarily in the centre. Placed within a ring of 102.5m radius, the seats would describe 12% in public ownership.[††] Each bench would have a brass plate with the name of each constituency. The order; a snake of geography (to be considered more carefully). A people's parliament, 73 seats, a gathering place, a rallying place without everyday.

References:

†   The Scottish Parliament Factsheet 1(http//www.scottishdevolution.org.uk/elections/factsheet.htm).
†† "Land Reform Policy Group" The Scottish Office, February 1998;
    (http//www.scotland.gov.uk/library/documents 1/Irpg01.htm).

Simon Beeson

Ayr
Carrick, Cumnock & Doon Valley
Clydesdale
Cunninghame South
Dumfries
Galloway & Upper Nithsdale
Roxburgh & Berwickshire
Tweeddale, Ettrick & Lauderdale
East Lothian
Midlothian
Livingstone
Linlithgow
Edinburgh Central
Edinburgh East & Musselburgh
Edinburgh North & Leith
Edinburgh Pentlands
Edinburgh South
Edinburgh West
Airdrie & Shotts
Coatbridge & Cryston
Cumbernauld & Kilsyth
East Kilbride
Falkirk East
Falkirk West
Hamilton South
Kilmarnock & Loudoun
Motherwell & Wishaw
Glasgow Anniesland
Glasgow Baillieston
Glasgow Cathcart
Glasgow Govan
Glasgow Kelvin
Glasgow Maryhill
Glasgow Pollock
Glasgow Rutherglen
Glasgow Shettleston
Glasgow Springburn

Clydebank & Mingavie
Cunninghame North
Dumbarton
Eastwood
Greenock & Inverclyde
Paisley North
Paisley South
Strathkelvin & Bearsden
West Renfrewshire
Central Fife
Dunfermline East
Dunfermline West
Kirkcaldy
North East Fife
North Tayside
Ochil
Perth
Stirling
Dundee East
Dundee West
Gordon
Aberdeen Central
Aberdeen North
Aberdeen South
Angus
Banff & Buchan
West Aberdeenshire & Kincardine
Argyll & Bute
Caithness, Sutherland & Easter Ross
Inverness East
Nairn & Lochaber
Moray
Ross, Skye & Inverness West
Western Isles
Shetland
Orkney
(Ayr)

A Proposal: flux?

Please mark clearly with a tick or a cross, in the appropriate box(es), your choice between each of the two options opposite and return a copy of the completed census with your details. All returned information will be treated with the strictest artistic integrity.

yes	no	option	yes	no	option	yes	no	option	yes	no	option
		up			heaven			latitude			hunter
		down			hell			longitude			hunted
		obtuse			ebb			first			work
		acute			flow			last			play
		red			buy			bridge			light
		white			sell			ferry			dark
		fish			reject			A			gold
		fowl			accept			B			silver
		edam			boil			yard			faith
		brie			freeze			metre			doubt
		adam			north			queen			fried
		eve			south			rooks			boiled
		bishop			divide			heads			iron
		knight			multiply			tails			driver
		sun			positive			in			long
		moon			negative			out			short
		sharp			ionic			watershed			chicken
		flat			doric			gardenshed			egg
		iron			control			wax			tide
		stone			panic			wane			edit
		bull			red			1707			stand
		bear			grey			7071			sit
		upland			vowel			ok			dolly
		lowland			consonant			uk			dolly
		odd			picture			fact			love
		even			words			fiction			hate
		him			pc			island			everything
		her			mac			peninsula			nothing
		full			flat			air			scissors
		empty			round			sea			paper
		armour			add			sauce			paper
		amour			subtract			vinegar			stone
		cut			left			organic			iron
		tear			felt			inorganic			dog
		blue			noughts			oil			wolf
		green			crosses			acrylic			flow
		forwards			latin			(			porridge
		backwards			greek			{			oats
		chalk			l			crime			comma
		cheese			0			punishment			punktum

name _____ occupation _____ age _____ sex _____

address _____

_____ nationality _____

return copy of completed census to: SEMPER FIDELIS 20 Cumberland Street Edinburgh EH3 6SA

Without Day: A Proposal

To take a photograph of the 129 MSPs on the occasion of the (re)opening of the Scottish Parliament in the building previously occupied by the General Assembly of the Church of Scotland. This is inspired by and will borrow from a painting completed by D. O. Hill in 1866 of the first General Assembly of the Free Church of Scotland in May of 1843. This 'Disruption' of the established Church was occasioned by the principle of reaffirming democracy and as a protest against patronage. The group portrait was made possible by Robert Adamson who, with Hill, employed the new technology of photography to make portraits of each of the ministers, from which Hill made the final painting.

Robin Gillanders

A Proposal for a Plaidie

A thread from a garment belonging to, or attributed to, every member of
the population of Scotland, from the dissolution of the Parliament in
1707, to its recall in 1999. The threads will be sorted for colour, washed,
carded and respun and woven into a ceremonial plaidie. This will be worn
on all such occasions of state as require the presence of the whole people.
The tartan would be designed by its makers, who would be drawn from all
over Scotland.

David Connearn

Without Day

This proposal to mark the occasion of a new Scottish Parliament involves the projection of plaids into the sky to produce a procession of tartan clouds over the city of Edinburgh.

In 1707, when the last Scottish Parliament was adjourned, there were many district tartans but few clan tartans. The district tartans reflected the dyes naturally available in the local landscape. The visit by George IV to Edinburgh in 1822 prompted the formalisation of clan tartans as clan chiefs who were invited to attend in formal attire confronted the definition of their cloth which might otherwise have rested quietly as numbers in a tartan weaver's book. There are now 6000 tartans and more are being invented all the time. The Scottish Tartan Society is making a computerised register of all plaids and can generate exquisite images based on thread counts (which are agreed) and colour specifications (which remain controversial).

Edinburgh's topography draws the sky into play in the experience of the city. Most weather advances from the Firth of Forth, and the cloudscape is perpetually changing. The height of the cloud base over Edinburgh is usually relatively low, between 1500 and 2500 feet, beneath planes circling at 4000 feet before landing. Sometimes the sky will be cloudless, and equally mists may occur when the cloud base drops to ground level, but more likely are days of high pressure when strata cumulus sheets present many cloud layers with breaks in all of them so that it is possible to observe distinct layers moving in different directions at different speeds, always resolved as a complex choreography. Also quite frequent are fine days when convection holds fluffy clouds in almost static formations overhead. These unpredictable ephemeral bodies would be beautifully articulated by tartan projections.

Laser projection allows for images to be perfectly focused whatever the height of the cloud base or the shape of the cloud, for there is no divergence of light. The tartan register could be used through a computer connection to produce the laser images. These could be projected in random sequences through a series of projectors so that the adjusted sky could be seen from all directions across the city. The parade of tartans in the sky would reflect the dynamic interplay of people on the ground and the symbolic convergence of representatives from all Scotland in its Parliament.

Jeanne Sillett

Day Without Day
A Box of Things for the Opening of the Scottish Parliament

A box, but not a mahogany covenanters' four-square:
one you might have put your milk teeth in,
tender buttons, stamps, nail-pairings, a small solar cell
and other incunabula of the life project. Also –

finder's keepers,
misbelief but no faith like this,
latifundian gorse,
sloes on the Galloway coast,
the pure spirit with sloes in it a year later,
earth from Theodosia,
memories of the Sabbath,
wee bit sangs,
cold unboiled peat-water in a can,
the sleeper's shape,
another Stevenson lighthouse,
the-Place-for-Hauling-up-Boats,
stripped willows,
the owl on your shoulder,
calling the saithe, in thirty variants,
silence's oxides,
mining by the light of incandescent fish-heads,
planking the evidence,
West Nile Street,
Hume lionised at d'Holbach's salon,
adjournment and dispersal,
knocking your pan in,
sine die,
the quiet before the opening of the seals,

First lay its meaning out flat. Then run your finger
over it, from one horizon to the next,
opening and closing, opening and closing it,
as if you were conceding that famous northern threnody
for squeeze-box and bag of guts –

a life-line,
a horse's skull,
a foetus with its thumb in mouth,
a knot,
a Viking long-ship,
a crannog,
a minister's falsers,
a day like any day,
a himberry,
a stone skimmed across water,
a bullet,
an egg-bed,
a rare walnut,
a whorlbane,
a washed-up tyre,
a garnet,
a cutty sark,
a queeny,
a fluky goal,
a dwam,
a poor-box shilling,
a shot star,
a stug of burning bush,
a fit-ba,
a V of migrating geese,
a lily-loch,

a dagger over words of the Older Scottish Tongue,
a grannie's hankie.

This is where memory begins
and things are trained to sound themselves
though you musn't listen too hard to the noise of time
in that emptiest of escapologists' boxes
for you won't hear a damn thing –

totemism,
box-wallahs of the continent,
the Streamers
miles and miles of not a lot,
Molucca beans cast up on the Western Isles,
the zaum of the wind in barbed wire,
Ossian read the bans,
the escueto style,
the deil as hero and comedian,
untamed words,
Europe's outerling nation,
life in the imperative of the future passive participle,
hochmagandy,
albino strawberries,
at the gates of the British Linen Bank,
an ear to the ground,
key words,
ease in its skin,
problems from Ibsen that swam across,
imported eau de Werther,
helleborine,
a hand cupped to an ear,
brave faces,

the Thane of Cawdor,
the odd sight of words becoming history,
spilt ink,
the race-tide on Luce Bay,
dates in the Hebrides,
charms,
post offices doubling as grocers,
bog asphodel;

not forgetting how many box owners, exhausted by time,
walked up their spines to find another box,
one bolted and locked though not by themselves –

Linnaeus on Jacob's Ladder,
a spatter of poppies,
soor plooms,
headed notepaper from the John Knox Institute, Geneva,
the Book of Esther,
Sir Mungo Lockhart of the Lee,
things hidden in plain sight,
Engineers Street,
oatmeal with everything,
Pictish Made Easy
St Kilda's parliament and the eighteen voices answering in chorus,
umbersorrow,
Edwin Muir in the bone factory,
the Old Firm,
forever under the pigeon,
our figurehead coming through the rye,
sheets of rain,
no more shortbread,
a tax on excessive use of the first person plural,

proceedings of the Scotia Bar,
Beuys on Rannoch Moor,
grey zones,
silence,
friends on the Faroes,
friends in Patagonia,
the Sargossa,
redcoats landing in France, again,
milkwort and bog-cotton,
my country doctor's box-coat bellying in the wind,
things as guarantors of belonging,
truly remarkable things,
facts unfurling,
quite unremarkable things.

Not a black box and certainly not Pandora's ironic box
(which wasn't a box anyway, but a jar)
with only hope inside, heavier than air, nor even a pill-box,
but a box of rain-and-lowering-sky picked up now
or later, added to, or taken away from, once or many times,
a box of the already-gone and the still-here –

Little Banff and Mid Whirr,
St Rollox,
The Whirlpool (a croft),
Sgurr Mor,
Rest and Be Thankful, again,
Rottenrow,
The Lynn of Lorn,
Little Float (another croft),
Strontian, driven through,
Brig o' Turk,

The Machars and the Rhins,
Loch Hope,
the ascent of the Law,
Hoy,
Rhum, Eigg and Muck,
two Scalpays,
the descent of Canisp,
Clova,
the Black Isle, in Tintin,
Man, from Lagvag,
Foula seen on a winter's day.

Things need cajoling before they can plead the life project
and enter a box's invitation to the labyrinth –
though things may not be worshipped or amassed except
by beginning curators, their boxes under pillows.

This, and this, and that as well –
not a list but a syntax;
less a chamber for goading the past
than a theatre of voices, in the words of its opening.

Iain Bamforth

A Proposal: Sherlock Holmes and Dr. Watson

Digital technology makes possible the recreation of moving images from photographs of the dead. This allows a magical film to be made telling the story of Sherlock Holmes and Dr. Watson. They are played impeccably by Norman MacCaig and Sorley Maclean.

MacCaig as Holmes is tall, lean, high-cheekboned, a little grey and tweedy in dress, quite spartan in comforts, intellectually self-sufficient but with a substantial personal library servicing his own esoteric and obsessive interests. He is determined in concentration and absolutely certain in his modes of analysis. His conclusions are reliable but some-what repetitive. He plays the fiddle but knows his limits. He requires a regularly self-administered drug, referring to the glass as 'the needle'. He is an expert on ash.

Maclean as Watson is much more rough-cast, hard-headed and serious-minded than his popular film image. He carries a wound from an old war in the east. He has an unpersuadable commitment to matters of human value and social worth. When they go into action, he carries the gun.

Both share senses of humour, generosities of spirit, depths of compassion and understanding, severities of belief. Occasionally, individually or mutually, their eyes will twinkle and gleam with recognitions.

They are called upon to investigate land-rent frauds, duplicitous government organisations, irresponsible authorities, cruel and twisted religions, violent crimes against the people and the hidden nature of reality.

In the end, the disguise of London is cast off and the city is revealed as Edinburgh. The Reichenbach Falls are in Sutherlandshire.

Moriarty is Henry Dundas.

A different kind of magic makes it possible to confirm that the film is approved by MacCaig, Maclean and Arthur Conan Doyle.

The film is immediately judged brilliant and increasingly loved by generation after generation.

It wins Oscars for all concerned but everyone boycotts Hollywood and in obeisant response the U.S. Government makes large sums of money available to support a major film industry in Scotland.

Some of the money is used to turn MacCaig's Folly in Oban into a Centre for Poetry, Film and the Performing Arts, with satellite links to all the world.

Alan Riach

A Proposal for a new Scottish Parliament

Iain Crichton Smith, George Mackay Brown and Norman MacCaig spend one day being alive again and writing poems on the walls of the biggest room in the Parliament.

The time spent being psychospiritual organisms has given them lots of inspiration and words flow from their pens like the self-replenishing Talisker bottle provided after dark.

After a night of magnificent tales first light returns them to their respective graves for a few more centuries.

Anna Strachan

A Proposal for Without Day

On the first day of the new Parliament in Scotland at 12 pm, Scotland will lose 2.63 minutes of daylight.

There are up to 16 hours of daylight in the summer months. Going on this assumption, the following calculations have been made the country will continue to lose 2.63 minutes daily for a calendar year, a total of 960 minutes. Scotland will be the only country affected; it will be 'without day'.

Pat Bray

from small spaces,   frozen tongues   a reminder of languages lost or dying or underused
corners,
which might
go unnoticed,
perhaps
private
places,
a shimmer,
a sparkle,
catches the eye
of someone
who has a voice.

the glitter

is one of

light on glass,

it requires

further investigation

a small glass
rectangular box
25.4mm x 76.2mm
sits
in its
unlikely corner

on closer
inspection
the curious
observer
will notice
that the box
is made of
microscope
slides
with one
opaque end

the opaque
squares
form
a five sided
cube
at
one
end
of
the
box

the
sixth side
is an
imaginary
wall
or an
opening
into the box

inside the box

half hidden

within the cube

is a tiny

and fragile

paper tongue

cast from clay

it appears

white

and cold

miniature

and

frozen   delicate paper to be   treated with care, a whispering reminder of all the unheard of languages without status   a reminder of the need to listen

to
those
without
a voice

and
to
those
forgotten
voices
inside

as
politicians
move
about
our
building
these
boxes
will refuse
to be forgotten
they will be
numerous
and placed to cause

light
to
play

on their surface,
casting shadows
and
shimmering seductively
fragile
whispers
barely
there
are
protected
by
microscope
slides
hinting
at the
need
for
closer
examination

for expansion of sound

reminding those with
power
to create a frame
for space
to
allow
the silenced
and forgotten
a place
to speak

where
tiny
whispers
can be heard
and made louder
till they own
their
potential
to
create
change

and silenced voices of yesterday, today and tomorrow   catriona macinnes

A Proposal for a New Scottish Parliament
A vigil

Davy Polmadie

A Proposal for an Inventory Wall Hanging

The New Scottish Parliament should establish a comprehensive inventory of the stock of native plants and animals in Scotland at the time of its inception (names to be noted in Gaelic and Scots as well as English or Latin); each species to be faithfully represented on a vast embroidered hanging set in the legislative hall, reminding members of our inheritance, its beauty, its fragility. The hanging will bear these lines from Iain Crichton Smith's poem 'The Village':

In these pictures / such light, such light!

The inventory to be reviewed biannually. If species are lost, the representative stitches must be unpicked, leaving the blank spaces, the traced outlines.

Anne Macleod

a proposal for a new scottish parliament
a dramatic historic event in scotland was
the disappearance of the large forests
scotland was famous for:

coille caledonia

to remember and to bring this back into
the actual politics i propose to bring the
names of all the forests that disappeared
anywhere in the parliament building on
a prominent place on the wall – be it cut
in stone, be it written in charcoal on the
wall. (many a forest was transformed to
charcoal to melt iron ore).

herman de vries

A Proposal: Without Day

For the new Scottish Parliament, I propose to design a fabric for all the chairs in the main chamber. I imagine that each parliamentarian will have a dedicated seat for the period they sit in office. These seats will be occupied for hours at a time when major issues are being debated.

The fabric will be very soft to the touch. It will be constituted by fine and smooth threads giving it the tactile properties of silk. A hand applied to the material will glide effortlessly over the seat as if there is an energy in the threads. This would result in a sensation to the palm of hovering – somewhere between touching and flying.

Each thread will be hollow and filled with fluon. This will enable the fabric to freeze once the seat is vacated by its occupant. When he/she returns to the seat, the fabric will once more become pliant.

The chairs will be connected to a sensory time switch at the entrance of the Parliament. This will register the arrival and departure of each member.

During the member's absence, the sensitive threads will hold, in negative, the form of the body as it last occupied the seat. The surface of the chair will appear to whiten with frost, rather like the surface of a lawn on a winter morning.

Under such conditions we are reminded of the last breath of air that blew, the last body that passed over. It is the lingering record of a displaced moment made visible – the trace of an arrested continuum.

Because of this displacement and the apparent suspension of time, a space is created for a special kind of contemplation.

So it will be in the Parliamentary chamber. When the house is not in session, a veil of dewy frost will take the place of the assembly – waiting, timeless . . .

Bryndís Snæbjörnsdóttir

A Proposal for Liberty Trees

A liberty tree will be planted in each village in Scotland.

J. P. MacMarra

A Proposal

RIVER TWEED

PRESSEN BURN

HALTER BURN

LIDDEL WATER

KERSHOPE BURN

RIVER SARK

in search of the kingfisher
crossing the river
crossing the border

Hans Waanders

A Proposal for a New Scottish Parliament

a
bright
orange
windsock
will be erected
in the centre of
every village,
town and city
of Scotland,
so that from
that day forth
the prevailing
wind will be
evident
to all.

Zoë Irvine

A Proposal for Early Day Parliamentary Bird-tables

It will be the duty of the Scottish Chancellor to set up bird-tables in the grounds of the New Scottish Parliament, one for each political party. The Chancellor will further provide each party with equal amounts of bird seed throughout the winter sessions: it will be each party's due responsibility to see that the birds in their area are fed at dawn, even through the Christmas Recess, and to keep a census of their feathered constituents.

The parties attracting the biggest number of birds, and the most unusual variety, will be awarded nesting boxes and free supplies of wood preserve for summer renovation. It is expected that the Parliamentary Birds will become a huge visitor attraction.

Anne Macleod

A Proposal, Chair

A large sculpture in the form of a chair with tall legs and a high back, five metres in height at its highest point. Proportions to suit an infant giant.

Unpolished bronze, with burnished detail.

The sculpture in all respects is to have the appearance of being wrought from a single piece, despite individually realised elements. Occasional pits and craters, blackening, sharp edges and crumplings suggest the work has endured forging, scorching and injurious but not annihilating accident.

A curving sensuousness remains.

The work is located at the heart of the new Parliament. Its absent occupant would be able to see all members, but the seat is marginally set back and off centre.

Each of the back legs has the shape of a mature Scots pine, with almost complete branchlessness in the lower two thirds of the trunk, then the characteristic broken rungs, then, as the legs touch and merge with the chair-back, the familiar crown-like canopy.

The front legs mimic the steel tubular pillars of an oil rig (not to scale with the back legs), rising to, and just piercing through, an oil platform. The platform also has the appearance of the large tray of a child's high-chair.

To the left, rooted to the platform, there is a tall stylised soft drink bottle, with spare cross-hatching that recalls tartan, rig engineering, and the metalwork of electricity pylons. Immediately next to this stands a stylised half-bottle of whisky, with detailing to suggest a broch's masonry.

The part of the platform closest to the chair merges on the right into an emblematic computer keyboard and monitor.

The monitor has markings at one side that suggest at the same time an embedded TV remote control and high-rise windows. It is connected by a wire – integral to the sculpture – to a 'mouse' that has a shape reminiscent of the dome at Dounreay power station. The back of the monitor, facing out from the chair towards the Parliament, appears to have undergone a metamorphosis so that is has the long, surly mouth of a fax machine. From this opening nearly two thirds of a blank, burnished sheet of bronze have emerged. The sheet is beginning to curl under its own weight.

The platform or tray is large enough to suggest an expanse of land or sea, in contrast to the technoclutter and towers at its edges. There are several undulations, some extreme and craggy, others more suggestive of a sea-like calm, some of a sea swell. Though the towers or bottles remain upright, the pieces of technological equipment look precarious and display a real risk of toppling the keyboard and mouse into the lap of any occupant, the monitor and fax over into the Parliament itself.

The arms of the seat are stylised versions of the Forth Rail Bridge (right) and the Erskine Road Bridge (left).

The chair back is high; throne-like. From behind, it has the austere look of a hydroelectric dam, but with a small number of intercut motifs: quietly stylised fossils of a thistle, of a salmon, and of a round-dial phone.

The base of the seat itself is plain, comfortable and worn looking. It is hinged at the back with hinges that appear to have survived perfectly intact. Two stout bolts at the front secure the seat base. Again, they appear to be in good working condition.

At the foot of the left back leg (that is, at the base of one of the Scots pines) a catheter-like tube emerges and becomes a braided hawser, leading away from the sculpture in a shallow curve. Finally, it transmutes into a snake-like body with the recognisable markings of an adder, beginning as a coil and lifting off of the Parliament floor as it does so. The raised adder's head, mouth open, also has some of the visual qualities of a large electric plug.

The chair has a ceremonial function. When the members have assembled, they are asked by the Presiding Officer: *"D'ye heed the chair?"* To take their place they must respond, *"Aye!"*. They are then asked the same in Gaelic: *"Na mhothaich sibh dhan chathair?"*, and, if they wish to take their place, must again reply in the affirmative, *"Mhothaich!"* Finally they are told by the Officer: *"The chair welcomes ye"*. Only once this is also said in Gaelic: *"Tha a' chathair a' cur fàilte oirbh"*, can the members be seated.

Richard Price

with thanks to Derick Thomson for the Gaelic translation

A Proposal: 110%

To enlarge by 10% every window, door, skirting-board, panel, light bulb, switch, socket, handle, cable, vent, fan, latch, clip, clasp, radiator, pipe, tile, tap, basin, plug, chain, towel, dispenser, bar of soap, roll of toilet paper, cistern, lid, seat and mirror in the toilets adjoining the Debating Chamber of the new Scottish Parliament.

Jim Hamlyn

My proposal is that a large clock with a number of special features would be erected in a central location in one of the main public areas of the new Parliament. This clock should incorporate a number of features which would elevate above the mundane.

It should tell both ordinary i.e. Greenwich mean time, and Edinburgh mean time, which is 12 minutes and 44 seconds behind G.M.T, to remind everybody that the Edinburgh Parliament marches to its own agenda, not that of London. The clock should strike both sets of hours and quarters, the 'London' hours being struck pianissimo and the 'Edinburgh' hours fortissimo, again to remind folks that Edinburgh has the controlling hand in many of Scotland's affairs.

The clock should also indicate the number of hours of daylight available each day, and should do this for the latitude of Shetland as well as for Edinburgh, just to remind people how big Scotland is, and how close parts of it come to the Arctic Circle. There should also be a dial to show the number of days remaining until the next election to Parliament; this will be a daily reminder to all MSPs that their office is temporary, granted by the will of the people, and subject to be terminated when they finally cock up too much.

The clock should also incorporate an Orrery, showing the dispositions of the main bodies of the Solar System, as a reminder that there is a bigger picture to be considered, and that decisions made in Edinburgh may have (unintended) planet wide, if not universal, reverberations.

Finally, the clock must be a mechanical clock, not a confection of electronic 'black boxes', and the workings of the clock must be exposed for all to see. This is so that like a properly accountable parliament, the workings of the clock's complex mechanism can be seen and understood by all who care to examine them without there being any secrets.

The expertise necessary to design and make such a monumental clock exists here in Scotland, and the creation of such a device would be a fitting public recognition of the high level of skill that Scotland continues to have in the mechanical arts.

Richard Ellam

A Proposal for a Computer Virus:

Running the country, are you?

The text is taken from Persius (*Satire 4*, line 1). The questioner (supposedly) is Socrates; the question comes therefore from the Edinburgh of the South.

The rest of the satire, which focuses on the greed and sexual appetites of politicians 'who turn pale at the sight of cash' and 'do whatever occurs to their pricks', suggests that little has changed. In this proposal, however, the question would appear, without explanation or attribution, as a virus infecting all communication and information systems of the Parliament. The phrase would appear within speeches reeling on auto-cues and typed up for distribution, within press releases, within memos and invoices, on letterheads, on receipts in the bars or cafes. It would insinuate itself also into election addresses from members of the Parliament to the voters, ensuring that the 'you' of the mocking question floats freely as the virus spreads.

The virus, if not a random interrogation, would perhaps be triggered by certain words appearing in titles, headings or texts; such words as 'Scottish' or 'Parliament' or 'democracy'.

A Proposal for the New Scottish Parliament

A room measuring approximately 4m x 5m x 3m should be set aside at the end of a quiet corridor. It should have even but discreet light, (natural or artificial) and a smallish door at the centre of one of the longest (5m) walls. The inside of the wall surrounding this door should be lined completely with 80mm thick charcoal grey foam rubber to deaden any acoustic. The 4m walls immediately to the left and right should be left blank, pure white. In the centre of the room should be one plain chair. On the 5m wall facing the door (also brilliant white) should be a single nail at the exact central point. Painted on an axis of 1.85m and also centred left and right should be a text in letters 21cm tall in bottle green. The text reads:

For the safe discharge of hypocrisy

Only one person may use the room at any one time.

Andrew Bick

Szuper Gallery at The New Scottish Parliament
Contemporary Art 2 / All Boys Programme 2000-2001:

Michael Stella
21 March – 24 April 2000
Reconstruction of Robert Morris *21.3*. In February 1964 Robert Morris performed at Surplus Dance Theatre in New York before a small audience. Clad in a neat gray suit and tie, he stood behind a podium, masquerading as an art historian for twenty minutes, as he lip-synched his own reading of the opening of Erwin Panofsky's essay 'Iconography and Iconology'.

Matthew Higgs
3 May – 11 June 2000
Matthew Higgs selects quotations from literary sources which describe a painting. He then asks different artists to imagine and repaint the literary model.

Heimo Zobernig
18 June – 27 July 2000
Heimo Zobernig restages a symposium which was originally held on the occasion of his solo exhibition in Nice in 1991. The different parts will be read by selected representatives from the Scottish art scene.

Philipe Thomas
6 August – 19 September 2000
Philipe Thomas executes a series of paintings for sale which subsequently will be signed by those who bought them.

Ernest T.
26 September – 2 November 2000
A retrospective (Paintings, Drawings and Objects).
Special film screening *Duck Soup* by The Marx Brothers.

Christoph Schlingensief
10 November – 19 December 2000
Deutschlandsuche '99. Christof Schlingensief travelled to Macedonia in
spring 1999 to visit the refugee camps. Two actors (Bernard Schütz and
Irm Hermann) from a Berlin theatre, impersonating the German
Chancellor Gerhard Schröder and his wife, accompanied him.

Alexander Brener
5 January – 14 February 2001
Gesture on 'Suprematism' by Kasimir Malevich, on loan from Stedelijk
Museum Amsterdam. Special film screening *The Third Generation* by
R. W. Fassbinder.

General Idea
22 February – 29 March 2001
Video screening *Shut the Fuck Up.*

A Proposal for an event

At about eleven o'clock in the morning a man appears at the bottom of
the Mound, at the centre of Edinburgh, to the right of the Royal Scottish
Academy, and starts to climb up the curve towards the meeting place of
the General Assembly, and temporary home of the Scottish Parliament.
He is entirely naked. His penis is perfectly visible, and in the course of his
walk will assume all the various guises that could characterise it: generally
limp, bouncing slightly with the rhythm of his pacing, thoroughly erect,
when he turns into the High Street to pass between the Sheriff Courts and
St. Giles' Church; now and again, chill and shrunken, as if its owner had
just been bathing in an upland loch, or were emerging from the showers
in a sports centre. When he first appears, the man is in his late 40s, not fat,
balding but with still dark hair and a serenely domed cranium. He could
be a businessman on the way to a meeting with his banker, were it not for
the total absence of clothing of any kind. Bystanders cannot quite believe
what they see and, as word spreads, small knots of onlookers form to
gape, generally on the opposite pavement to the one where the man is
walking. Two policemen get ready to arrest him. What stops them in their
tracks is the way his aspect changes. Without it being possible to
distinguish intermediate stages, yet without a trace of abruptness, he is in
turn a child of seven, an adolescent with light down barely perceptible on
his chin, and an old man leaning on a stick, who has to drag his weight
along. At one point there is a wreath of rowan berries round his temples.
At another he wears the headgear and carries the insignia of an African
chief. The pale light of a Scottish sun trickles up and down his burnished
skin like water. Going past the Nethergate and the place where the Scottish
Poetry Library used to be, he is a punk clothed in black from neck to foot,
festooned with spikes and rings and wearing an orange wig. It is not
possible to see his genitals, which this radical puritan outfit solicitously

conceals. Halfway down the Canongate, all of a sudden he is in drag. Passers-by reflect that they had not realised how shapely his thighs were and, though his breasts are a little too prominent to be convincing, and his legs as seen through the slit in his purple dress have obviously been shaved, cannot help bursting into spontaneous applause. By the time he reaches the new parliament building, he is naked again. He does not pause when confronted by the outer stone facing and melts into it, leaving behind an imprint of his body shape which will prove impossible to wash off, and will be pointed out to generation after generation for centuries to come . . .

Christopher Whyte

A Proposal for Without Day

I propose an Archive for those years that were 'without day'.

The Archive would be dovetailed into the new parliamentary building. The Archive deposits would comprise bound Volumes (Vols 1 – 293), record of Parliamentary Proceedings for the years 1707 – 1999.

Each Volume, a day book for the year, would contain 365 (366 for leap years) feather light pages. Volume 1 (for 1707) and Volume 293 (1999) would have minuted proceedings, the rest would remain void.

Housed in the dark, without day, at any one time, any or all of these volumes could be lifted and placed, opened to the light, on plinths about 1.5 m. in height.

In addition fans electrically plugged to each plinth, as numerous as the volumes, would whirr. With light and airing, the books would give vent to their tales and transform.

Fan Tails.

A Proposal: The Inner Islands

A competition is to be offered every three years for the best depiction of an imaginary Scottish island, complete with bearings, place-names, flora, fauna, recipe book of the islanders' favourite food, local industries, a poster from the island's Entertainment Committee, a four page edition of the *Island Enquirer* and so forth. Postcard views of the best virtual island are devised and made available for sale. Each postcard entitles the bearer to a 50% discount on the ferry which sails closest to the point in the sea where the island ought to be. Photographs may be taken and crofting rights bought. All profits from postcard sales and television rights are used to support real projects on real Scottish islands, whether inhabited or uninhabited.

James McGonigal

Katanes Ting

The Scottish Parliament demonstrates devolution of power to Scotland as a whole, enabling more effective action to be taken in response to the country's needs and desires. A logical progression of the self-determination would be to create a smaller unit of power to respond to and enhance Caithness.

The unit would be established heeding relevant examples throughout the world, e.g. Norwegian Kommunes, in addition to closer examples such as the powerful island council of Shetland. An emphasis would be placed on responding to the distinctive local culture, primarily Norse, and as a strong statement of this the unit would be called *Katanes Ting* (Norse meaning: Caithness Assembly).

The *Katanes Ting* would embody the accountable local power structure of traditional Norse governance in the area, taking the Earldom of Orkney as an example. Links to areas of common interest would be forged, such as the previously mentioned Orkney and Shetland, giving these areas a strong voice in the Scottish Parliament, throughout the North Atlantic and Europe. A specific example of this would be to reestablish Scrabster as a destination on the Smyral ferry route, which encompasses Bergen, Lerwick and Torshavn. The Smyral would be promoted by the *Katanes Ting* as a conduit of Caithnessian exports and a source of imports, e.g. tasty Faroese puffin to celebrate St Olav's Day.

The *Katanes Ting* should also advocate more beneficial twinning with other areas, such as between Thurso and Reykjavik, which would reinforce the benefits of mutual trade and cross-cultural exchange. Other areas within Scotland could work with the *Ting* to ensure shared benefits. In the area of transport the Far North Railway Line could be improved by Sutherland's equivalent assembly working with the *Katanes Ting*.

The principles on which the *Ting* would function would be those of promoting prosperity and vitality in the area, whilst encouraging sustainable development and penalising environmental pollution. Attention would be paid to the unique nature and culture of Caithness, while retaining a positive perspective on development.

The *Katanes Ting* would be served by a speaker, whose responsibility it would be to represent the *Ting* in the Scottish Parliament and ensure the *Ting's* founding principles were adhered to. In the spirit of historical context, should the speaker neglect their duties they would be swiftly removed and replaced with a more effective person. The speaker would also report to the *Ting* on progress in Caithness itself, in such fields as tourism, export or education.

The *Katanes Ting* would be a brave step in self-determination for Caithness, combining the lessons of historical precedent and a vision of future democracy. The formation of a Scottish Parliament was only the beginning of redressing the imbalance of our centralised constitution. The next step is to establish the *Katanes Ting* . . .

Corrina Thomson

A Proposal for a New Scottish Parliament

My proposal for the new Scottish Parliament concerns the mythological emblem of Scotland, the spider. It is not possible to be certain of the particular kind of spider that inspired Robert the Bruce to be persistent; so I will include every kind of spider which lives in Scotland in my proposal.

At the moment that the new Scottish Parliament is opened every door into the building will be thrown open and entered by a 'Spider Porter', each of whom will carry a box containing a male and female spider. There will be one box for every variety of spider known in Scotland: 'Dwarf Spiders', 'Harvestmen', 'Scaffold Web Spiders', 'Long Jawed Orb Weavers', 'Jumping Spiders', 'Nursery Web Spiders', 'Money Spiders', 'Ground Spiders', 'Water Spiders', 'Spitting Spiders', 'Six Eyed Spiders', 'Lady Bird Spiders', 'Funnel Weavers', spiders from the Cairngorms, even the rare 'Wolf Spiders' who live on the high plateau of the Highlands, all will be brought into the building and released.

The spiders will begin to spin webs throughout the building. Their continuous activity will inspire the parliamentarians who will recognise that one of them is the actual descendent of the original Scottish Spider, and all are working in a spirit of tireless idealism.

The spiders' project will be to multiply and clothe the building in a vast web of aesthetic architecture. Their vision is of a world without the need for National Parliaments, long after the building has decayed, they imagine simply their commemoration in the imitative webs woven by human collaborative activity across the globe.

Realisation:

This proposal could be presented as an exhibit using:

A list of all the spiders introduced into the building.

A photograph of a 'Spider Porter' releasing a pair of spiders[1] from a spider box.

A pair of white cotton gloves as worn by the 'Spider Porter' in the photograph.

A spider box with label containing a photograph of the particular spiders natural habitat and a map of its web.

More Ambitiously:

A model of the building in 2770 could be made, by which time the fabric of the building will have decayed and the structure will be clothed in a spider web.[2] This model would provide a dematerialised counterbalance to any actual model of the new building.

---

1   The spiders featured in the photograph would be dwarf spiders, chosen because they will not be visible and therefore will not cause alarm to any arachnaphobic viewers who come across the exhibit by accident.
2   To be lit by diachroic spotlights.

A Proposal

To make friends with the secretary to the First Minister by writing a series of letters to her. I would write these letters whilst working as a secretary myself. They would describe the situation I was in, of writing about people I do not know and will not meet, for someone who only knows my name. These letters would be written in shorthand.

Proposal for a New Scottish Parliament

For the first year of the new Scottish Parliament each city and town within Scotland would be supplied with an electronic L.E.D. text based sign which would be directly linked to the new Scottish Parliament. The purpose of these 'debatometers' would be to relay the decibel level currently being generated by the members in the debating chamber of the new Scottish Parliament. The 'debatometers' would be of a design that is already commercially available and they would be situated on top of appropriate public buildings such as libraries or council offices. The largest 'debatometer' would be situated at the new Parliament itself.

Paul Dignan

A Proposal

Our Dynamic Earth will occasionally be mistaken for the
Scottish Parliament.

The Scottish Parliament will occasionally be mistaken for
Our Dynamic Earth.

A Proposal: Tuning In

Materials: P. A. amp, speakers and sound.

A series of specially constructed speakers will be located at specific points within the main chamber. The recording of a lighthouse fog signal will be played at regular intervals. The overlapping sound structures of the plangent (the fog horn) and the persistent (the continuous sound in the room) will set in play a whole series of narratives and evocative images. The outside will be re-sized and re-interpreted from the inside. After a while listening and looking, the regularity of the sound and the gaps between them will be hypnotic and an echo will begin to wedge itself in the silence.

When the sound is played, the construction and placement of the speakers will create a harmonic resonance and gentle vibration in tune with the building, and the silence will be felt.

Louis Nixon

A Proposal for a New Scottish Parliament

In the new Scottish Parliament building I would love to see something for the visually impaired. Around the building, I would like to see large Braille texts, set as long lines, above handrail height, with verses of Scottish poetry, both the well known and contemporary. For the sighted there would be a small text next to it, but it would be firstly for those who read Braille. I would like to see these placed around the building, in foyer spaces and in lengthy corridors.

Lilian Cooper

Without Day: A Proposal for the Scottish Parliament.

Form a coalition with the stars . . .

Ross Birrell

A Proposal for An Hour

A parliament is a talking shop.
There will be people of all sorts –
Members and also the public
who will come to speak, to persuade,
to bludgeon, to deceive or to ingratiate.

An event which I propose would be a meeting
called An Hour
at a certain time
at a certain place
for that certain duration,
where Parliamentarians and outsiders
would be together
in silence.

Seemingly doing nothing.
And yet in some sense in communion.

The setting should be one of the fine rooms that the Parliament
will have. It will surely have a serious quality coupled with
some idea of innovation.

Although this has the flavour of a Friends' meeting,
no one would speak,
even though they might feel inclined.

Perhaps we would be attending to our experience
but perhaps also thinking.

Some might think about the Glory of Scotland,
some about its new responsibilities,
some about the other people there,
some about mundane daily worries, some about nothing.

It would simply be 'a being together'.

At the end of the time allotted
one might want to clap
or perhaps just to melt away.
An hour of silence with others,
is something unusual.

I think it couldn't help doing something to us, for us.

Halla Beloff

A Proposal for Without Day

This proposal involves a response to day through transposing variations in sunlight into sound. Bright sunlight will therefore be transposed into sound in the upper register, and dark stormy overcast conditions; sound in a lower register through to the dark rumbling double bass before the storm. The transposition of sunlight into sound will be accomplished through two audio kinetic sculptures that continually monitor the sunlight and rotate plectrums over strings to produce sounds. They will be tuned to the key of E, the key of light. These sculptures rely on the use of two distinct levels of technology, the ancient plucking of strings and the use of the latest photoelectric technology to monitor the sunlight and rotate the plectrums over the strings. The two sculptures will be located at either end of the Scottish mainland, one in the south and the other in the north, though the latter might also be positioned on the most northerly point of the most northerly island. The sound these sculptures create will be transmitted by satellite to the Scottish Houses of Parliament so that the two sounds, the two qualities of sunlight, the two extremities of the country combine and make music in the administrative centre.

This is not a new idea, and it is not the first time it has been associated with government. It is recorded that in ancient Thebes a statue of king Memnon made sounds at the rising and setting of the sun that were similar to the sounds made by a stringed instrument. As with King Memnon, the intention in this proposal is to develop innovative systems that lead to new aesthetic experience and possibly to new areas of awareness.

Andrew A. Stonyer

A Proposal

Rainbow
Lighthouse
Telescope

An upturned telescope,
central and monumental,
on Calton Hill
    transmutes
at the turn of an era
 into a lighthouse
whose bright beam of light,
    focusing outward[1]
through a bank of lenses,
shines above deep foundations,
    a kind of starlight,[2]
with lights guiding
    and aiding safe navigation,
    lights also warning of
unseen dangers
    beneath the surface
of life
in city streets,
    on Scotland's seas,
in the Highlands,
    in the islands,
villages, towns,
    work places,
    open spaces and homes,

warning of hazards in the water,
 of threats in the ether and
 risks beyond these shores,
in these new lights of
 seven colours of the rainbow
 for seven days and nights of the week,
 with light painting also by degrees
 the time ball
the sphere set high
 which rises and falls
marking the middle of each day
in time with the boom of the
 one o'clock gun
rolling downhill
 from the castle ramparts
 to the water's edge
& under the clockwork globe
 the rainbow beam
 swoops round the source
 setting every edifice in proper lights,[3]
casting an arch of promise
beneath which
 the work of a new parliament is done,
under the glow of the hill
where for years
the lightkeepers
 held their vigil[4]
beckoning this sea change
holding tight for a

people coming together
with multiple angles
    of incidence
    angles of refraction,
    reflection
    & ultimate emergence
until we are ready
to rebeam
    into the blue
all colours
    all people
of all ages,
in all areas
    concentrated into the white beams
that cross confidently
into the bright blue sky for Scotland.

1   Donald Dewar (1999) in the foreword to *A Guide to the Scottish Parliament: The Shape of Things to Come*: 'instead of turning inward and emphasising the past, we should focus outward to the wide world and the challenges of the future.'

2   Francis Bacon (1617): 'Lighthouses are marks and signs . . . being a matter of high and precious nature, in respect of salvation of ships and lives and a kind of starlight in that element.'

3   Lord Cockburn (1849) in *A letter to the Lord Provost on the best ways of spoiling the beauty of Edinburgh*: 'The Calton Hill is the glory of Edinburgh . . . That sacred mount is destined, I trust, to be still more solemnly adorned by good architecture, worthily applied. So as the walks and the prospects, and the facility of seeing every edifice in proper lights, and from proper distances, be preserved, and only great names and great events be immortalised, it cannot be crowned by too much high art.'

4   Robert Louis Stevenson, from *The Light-Keeper*: 'Quiet and still at his desk / The lonely Light-Keeper / Holds his vigil'.

Elspeth Murray

A Proposal for Without Day

They have been placed randomly in the walls of the Parliament building, and if one wasn't looking they'd be easily missed. In various rooms and corridors, at shoulder height, are small copper portals about 4 inches in diameter. They are hardware from another time; we can easily imagine butlers once being summoned through these same mouthpieces, but these days their function is much more cathartic. Today, we see MSPs throughout the building taking a minute or two out of their busy days to quietly speak into them. Some self-consciously mutter into the holes from behind the pages of newspapers before quickly moving on, others unashamedly read through long lists scribbled down during their last meeting.

If we get closer to the confessors and listen just over their shoulders we understand the importance of the work being done. They are moaning for Scotland. Their grievances cover everything; the English, traffic congestion, football . . . it's an endless drizzle from a cloud of discontent. They complain until they're breathless then walk away cleansed. What they work towards is a Scottish pride that is truly pride, and in helping the national consiousness evolve, they moan the moan of patriots.

And if we follow the intricate network of tubes that carry these words away, they all lead to a basement room that even the MSPs don't know about. In it, 61 year old Dougie Collins listens to the politician's complaints as they enter large glass bottles. Dougie seals and labels the bottles before sending them to a storage facility in Leith. Sometimes he gets bored and thinks how it might be nice to exhibit the bottles in an art gallery or maybe lob a couple at the front door of Number 10 Downing Street (just a couple), but mostly he's just glad he doesn't work at the library any more.

Brock Lueck

A Proposal for a Continuous Sunrise

On the night before the Winter solstice prior to the opening of the Scottish Parliament, just before dawn an aircraft takes off from Leuchars and flies at the same speed as the dawn, travelling seven kilometres south of the 56th parallel, just ahead of the sunrise, continuously videoing it.

In villages, towns and cities along this latitude beneath the flight path, large video screens are set up in public places, squares, parks, gardens etc., facing west.

The transmission from the aircraft of the continuous sunrise is relayed in real time and shown on the screens in this circle of settlements around the globe. People gathering in these places during the night, will be able to watch the dawn approaching. The aircraft, crossing different weather systems and landscapes, will show the sunrise in varying circumstances; with, for instance, a constantly changing horizon.

At a particular moment in each place, the sky behind the screen showing the approaching sun-rise will begin to brighten, and the assembled people will hear the sound of the approaching aircraft. They see the image on the screen and the sky before them coincide as the aircraft passes overhead.

The proposed flightpath will pass over many places, including Garraway in Manitoba, just north of Buffalo Narrows in Saskatchewan, Desmarais in Alberta, Rolla and Farmington in British Columbia, Hyde in Alaska, north of Kamchatsk in Kamchatskaya Oblast, Nagornyy in the Yakutskaya Republic, Nelaty and Muya in Chitinskaya Oblast, Tomsk, just north of Kazan and Moscow in Russia, Liepaja in Latvia, just south of Helsingborg in Sweden, just north of Horsens in Denmark, and finally over a huge screen set up in front of the new seat of government in Edinburgh.

Fred Scott

Late but hopefully not too late I send you my proposal for the proud Scottish Parliament

Basically there are two installations which involve so called 'new media'. As we both know it was a Scotsman who invented television (and an American who made money out of it) so 'new media' is per definition already something Scottish.

Okay. There is one work for the foyer (if there is one) which is a sort of sound installation – but more like a mini radio drama. The work will be interactive and refers to the frequency of visitors.

I will record the voices of all sorts of Scottish people and ask them always the same question: *"What or whom would you vote for most in life?"*. (I am sure this isn't grammatically correct but this can be fixed I guess). There will be no special choice of people; everybody who comes along will be asked.

Now I will split the answers in two parts (in a tone studio); one part will be just *"I vote"*, and the other part will be just the subject they said they would vote for most. The installation will now consist of infrared light barriers which if you pass them in the foyer are generating *"I vote"* like a whisper. The *"I vote"* phrase comes up as people pass. The phrases are always in a different voice or accent and should not repeat too early. There will be more than one speaker so you will hear a whisper of more than one voice.

Infrared barrier number two is or should be in front of the actual entrance to the parliaments chamber. There is the same system but now you will hear the different answers as one word voice mails.

I call this work maybe *choice* or simply *"VOTE!"*

The other work will be inside the Parliament and is a video projection above the heads of the politicians. The projection should be permanent and will be updated from time to time. The film of the images shown are very simple. They are short video portraits from Scottish people made all over the country. They shouldn't talk but the heads can move or smile. The portraits will overdub very smoothly to the next portrait. This has to be very slow. Again there will be no special choice of people. A local Scottish TV company will from time to time make more of those portraits and upgrade the video installation with new images.

The whole character of the video beam is a very relaxed and calm one.

I call this work maybe *PEOPLE* .

A Proposal for a Satellite/National Mood Cube

In time for the opening of the new Scottish Parliament building, negotiations should be entered into with Russia for the rental, in perpetuity, if not outright purchase, of its illuminating satellite. You will recall how this satellite was intended, by means of remarkable mirrors, to cast eternal daylight upon a little Siberian enclave to cheer up the populace who are used to interminably dark winter days (and pretty short-lived summers). This project having been aborted, the entrepreneurial Scots should bid to take it over with a view to re-aligning its solar reflector and focusing permanent light – perhaps not celestial, but the next best thing – upon the glorious structure in which so much of our collective future is invested.

As a natural development of this, the light in which our Parliament will forever bask could be treated with filters mounted on the satellite, to reflect the prevailing national disposition – red for belligerent; green for wishing we were once again annexed to England, and so forth – thus functioning as a national mood-cube.

Douglas Lipton

In the new Scotland it is important that trade be increased to facilitate greater wealth and employment.

This proposal to increase trade would, at a stroke, increase employment for cartographers, printers, solicitors, signmakers, publishers, librarians, graphic designers, computer programmers, foundrymen, surveyors, town planners, historians, administrators, drivers, secretaries, clerks, public officials and the manufacturers of aluminium ladders.

Secondary layers of employment would also increase.

This increase in trade would be achieved by attaching the prefix 'trade' to every place name, throughout the land, which is named 'Union'. So Union Street in Aberdeen would become Trade Union Street and the Union Canal would, forever after, be known as the Trade Union Canal.

Donald Urquhart

A Proposal: New Day
A site work in two complementary parts

A light-work delineating a line through the zone of the deep geological fault; 'possibly a horizontal strike slip', which runs from East to West through the Holyrood site. This fibre – optic light work will enter the Parliament building along the landscape link to the park, through the public plaza, running diagonally through the inside at garden level and out again into the grounds towards the West. It will signal the existence of the fault, mediating it and transforming it into a ribbon of light.

The fibre will be illuminated by digitally controlled and synchronised light sources fuelled by solar energy, creating a sense of movement through subtle shifts choreographed along its length, and programmed to reflect differing times of day and night and the seasons of the year. The dynamics of the earth which created the fault and the constantly moving geological structure of the earth as a living entity will be signalled. Multiple readings are posited.

Secure installation procedures will be followed, the fibre optic cable being cast into the ground and protected by panels of annealed glass, adhering to the highest safety specification 'for pavement use'. Life expectancy is good for the fibre and light source maintenance is easy.

A sound-work which will operate after the business of the day is finished and the buildings are closed. The chambers of the Parliament will be washed throughout with sounds designed to cleanse the buildings of static energies. Each new day will thus be freshly engaged with by all who work within or enter, the Parliament. During the night security and maintenance staff may experience this shifting sound environment, and snatches of it will be heard occasionally by nocturnal passers-by.

These sounds will be worked from a compilation of natural and electronically fabricated sources and transmitted to high level acoustic specifications. Some will be sublime.

Wisdom, vision and compassion will flourish.

Rose Frain, Artist
In consultation with Norman E. Butcher, Geologist; Mike Hall, Composer;
Kevan Shaw, Lighting Consultant.

A Proposal to Rearrange the Map of Scotland According to the Relative Positions of 'Scottish' Towns and Landmarks in South Africa.

The following places would need to be moved:

Aberdeen
Aberfeldy
Balmoral
Braemar
Dundee
Elgin
Fraserburgh
Glencoe
Kinross
Orkney
Sutherland

Several new towns would be created, including:

Campbell
Clanwilliam
McGregor
Robertson
Scottburgh

On the rearranged map of Scotland, Dundee would therefore be approximately 560 miles north-east of Aberdeen, but only six miles east of Glencoe. Orkney would be about 75 miles west-south-west of Balmoral, whilst Clanwilliam would be located roughly 110 miles west of Sutherland which, in turn, would be almost 200 miles due west of Aberdeen.

Ben Macdhui (1309m) would remain one of the country's highest mountains, but at a height of 3002m, in accordance with its South African counterpart.

The new parliament would be relocated in Caledon, a small town near the south 'coast' of Scotland, approximately 150 miles due south from Clanwilliam.

Roger Palmer

Without Day: A Voyage

Beat and 'scribe Sea Bounds, Coast – Kingdom of Fife:

Sleepless Inch
Upper Tay, suspended
time without day
Canoe to Carpow
then follow
East Coast Sailing Directions
Newburgh
Balmerino
Newport, Wormit
Tayport
Eden
St Andrews
Double North Carr
Isle of May
Crail
Anstruther
Pittenweem
St Monans
Elie Ness
Elie and Earlsferry
Largo, Leven
Wemyss
Dysart

Raith
Kinghorn
Pettycurr
Burntisland
Inchcolm
Halfo'er
To Aberdour
Mortimer's Deep
Inverkeithing
North Queensferry
Bride of the Kingdom
Then
Shoot the bridges (2x)
follow 'Lothianshore'
Cramond
Granton
Newhaven
Leith
Dip to New Scottish Office
Attend afternoon signal from Calton Hill
reset chronometer
restart time
recover the day

Stephen Hughes and Graham Rich

'Fear a bhata', 'The Boatman': a six minute happening

A plain wall, possibly curved. A continuous moving image of the surface of the sea is projected onto the entire wall from two points. The voice of a woman sings, unaccompanied, an old Highland song, 'Fear a bhata', 'The Boatman', in Gaelic and then in English, to a traditional melody.

It is a song about promises and betrayal. Here are three verses (in a 19th century translation from the Gaelic):

How often haunting the highest hilltop
I scan the ocean thy sail to see;
Wilt thou come to-night, love? Wilt come to-morrow?
Wilt ever come, to comfort me?
Fhir a bhata, na horo eile,
Fhir a bhata, na horo eile,
Fhir a bhata, na horo eile,
O fare ye well, love, where'er ye be.

They call thee fickle, they call thee false one,
And seek to change me, but all in vain;
No, thou art my dream yet throughout the dark night,
And every morn yet I watch the main.
    Fhir a bhata, etc.

Dost thou remember the promise made me,
The tartan plaidie, the silken gown,
The ring of gold with thy hair and portrait?
That gown and ring I will never own.
 Fhir a bhata, etc.

A Proposal: Vital Peripheries

Much sensory experience comes from the extremities of the body
fingertips; toes; nose. So an administration must recognise the sound
political value of paying due attention to information and experience
gathered towards the limits of the area of its jurisdiction.

It is possible that a Parliament, placed at some distance from its
sensory limits, may need some reminder of their significance. In a climate
where words will inevitably hold sway, echoes of peripheral areas must
have potency beyond language. Pibroch; mouth-music; and tunes for
harp, fiddle and flute have proven to be efficient storage devices for such
power.

First we must visit points of our geography in a series of way points –
all islands located at extreme peripheries. The following are proposed:

Isle of May	*56 degrees 11 minutes North*
	2 degrees 34 minutes West
North Ronaldsay	*59 degrees 23 minutes North*
	2 degrees 22 minutes West
Unst	*60 degrees 49 minutes North*
	0 degrees 46 minutes West
Soay (St Kilda)	*57 degrees 50 minutes North*
	8 degrees 38 minutes West
Orsay	*55 degrees 40 minutes North*
	6 degrees 30 minutes West

The First Minister should proceed, in the company of a selected
musician to these locations. The experience should prompt meditation
and, in the case of the musician, the recording of a suitable composition.
Neither the First Minister nor the musician is necessarily required to pass
water on the particular islands. The territories are already adequately

mapped. Passage in a Scots-built surface-vessel is preferred but aircraft travel is permitted.

Musicians who have shown a degree of innovation along with a sound grasp of where they're coming from are sought. The following persons are proposed:

Savourna Stephenson	*for Isle of May*	*harp*
Martyn Bennett	*for North Ronaldsay*	*pipes*
Aly Bain	*for Unst*	*fiddle*
Mary Smith	*for Soay*	*mouth-music*
Sean O'Rourke	*for Islay*	*flute*

Recordings of the resulting compositions are to be incorporated into landscaping works around the completed new building. A sample of rock collected from each of the islands is to be placed as a station on the true compass bearing to these islands from the centre of the Parliament. A switching mechanism will enable visitor or worker to hear the relevant piece of music which should not be longer than 5 minutes duration.

Ian Stephen

A Proposal

The metaphor of the boat-shaped buildings in Miralles' first design for the new Scottish Parliament, is completed with the addition of Port Letters and Fishing Numbers to each building. The Letters and Numbers are upside down or the right way up in relation to the viewer as the configuration of the various 'hulls' suggest. Scottish ports are indicated.

Ian Hamilton Finlay

A Proposal for a Pigeon Petition Service

White homing pigeons are reared in a doocot in the grounds of the new Parliament, and sent out regularly to regional centres and old county towns. Petitions from individual citizens or groups can be pithily expressed and sent by pigeon to Edinburgh. Returning pigeons are filmed flying in, for the evening news reports, and petitions are to be responded to as a matter of urgency by the relevant minister. Petitions are limited to one per person per year. Each pigeon has a blue rectangle of harmless dye painted on its chest, with a white saltire of feathers left in the centre, or just left of centre.

James McGonigal

A Proposal: When A causes B

The bronze sculpture of David Hume (1711–76) sited on the corner of Bank Street, adjacent to the Parliament Square, should be taken down from its plinth and broken into pieces. As a result of this process the sculpture will be transformed from a complete, if static, image of the man into a loose assembly of fragments lying besides its empty plinth. At this stage of the process the fragments will still bear reference to the figure itself. The larger pieces would then be methodically broken up into pieces small enough to be loaded into crucibles which should then be placed, one after the other, into the flames of a portable furnace.

Once each crucible has reached the correct melting temperature for bronze, the molten metal would be poured into a set of previously prepared identical moulds. The number of moulds filled will be dictated by the amount of bronze taken from the original sculpture. Whilst there may be some small amount of loss during the firing due to the nature of the process and the presence of impurities in the original metal, in essence the newly cast objects should reflect the weight and, therefore, bear some of the gravity of the original.

After the metal has been allowed to cool the moulds can be broken open. Each opened mould reveals its contents – a series of identical spheres about the size of billiard balls. Each sphere would be cleaned of all the mould marks and rendered to as pure a sphere as is possible. Finally they should be polished to a high shine.

On completion (a process that would take an un-specified number of days working on site) each sphere should then be thrown onto the open space of Parliament Square and allowed to remain where it has landed or rolled. This process would be repeated until all the spheres lie randomly where they have come to rest on the square, each ball taking its own position in relation to the others on the ground.

The work would then be allowed to lie undisturbed, except for those movements of the spheres, which are effected by events in the square – the intentional or unintentional displacement of the objects caused by passers-by etc.

The plinth with its title HUME should be retained, but kept empty, to preside over and bear witness to the subsequent events that effect the positions of the spheres.

Jim Harold

The original phrase 'Without Day' was used at the standing-down of the 1707 Parliament to describe the absence of a date for its re-constitution. It is essentially pessimistic, an ending. But here we are with a new Parliament a new beginning in front of us, and with a need to express that new beginning with optimism.

The Parliament must bring with it hope for the revitalisation of our Nation. It is to be situated at Holyrood in a building whose architecture sets out to connect with our landscape and history. Nearby Calton Hill was one of the other sites considered and a great many people feel drawn to it as a special place. Edinburgh may be laid out below but we are also drawn to the wonderful views out to the landscape of Scotland. On a fine, breezy day there you can see clearly and see far. The echoes of the Acropolis in Athens have shaped our built response to it, but there are also echoes there of the Allthing, the Icelandic parliament, oldest in Europe, which met in the open air. It is extraordinary that in the centre of Edinburgh there should be a place which feels like it connects so well, both directly to the landscape beyond the City and to our central democratic traditions.

Dominating Calton Hill is the built fragment of a Parthenon that was to have been the National Monument. This proposal is to "complete" the National Monument in a radically altered and updated form to celebrate the establishment of the Holyrood Parliament, making a new Monument for us and our future.

It is proposed that the shape of the monument – its footprint – is filled-in with a dense field of around one hundred tall, narrow flags, the flagpoles reaching as high as the monument's columns. The flags themselves are roughly one foot wide but they reach from the top of their poles nearly down to the ground. There is a tradition of such things in the

Himalayas. There each flag carries the text of a prayer, and the flags whip and crack in a wind that blows the prayers out across the land.

On our flags would be written texts gathered from Scottish schoolchildren setting out their hopes for the renewal of Scotland. Every school in the Nation would have a contribution. Calton Hill would become a democratic broadcasting station receiving messages from our young for the Parliament below and then sending them out across the land on the wind.

An aside:
Without Day, in its original form, is a bleak description of the disengagement of Government from Nation. Used here it has been transformed into a term of approval, the disengagement of an artistic proposal from the temporal limitations of actually realising it seen as somehow virtuous. I do not agree. It is true that Art exists on a different plane from the ordinary (and extraordinary) World around us. But this does not mean that Art is separate from the World it only exists in reference and relation to it, as celebration or meditation.

If I was allowed to write one hope on the flags it might be that our Art might learn to re-engage, at one and the same time with the reality of our beings and with the transcendent around us. So, yes, I would like to realise this proposal.

Malcom Fraser

A Litany: For Us, For You, For Them

The electronic technology for this proposal is feasible, if complex. It would be based on an existing text, which has already been used successfully in a similar way, although only for transient oral presentation.

There would be no visual element, other than possibly a discreet plaque somewhere nearby, and could be done with a number of different voice recordings, or a single voice.

There would be three synchronised "tracks". The first would repeat in sequence *"for us"* . . . *"for you"* . . . *"for them"*. The second, alternating with the first, would repeat a series of 28 substantives (nouns). The third, alternating also after the second, would repeat a sequence of 59 (or other prime number) of modifying phrases or clauses, resulting in sequences of the character of:

> *"for us . . . a time . . . beyond silence"*
> *"for you . . . a place . . . and there is no mistake"*
> *"for them . . . a hope . . . against mere limitation"* etc.

Each sequence would thus be syntactically coherent, with a slight pause between each.

Thus, assuming these figures, there would be 3 times 28 times 59 combinations (e.g. total of 4956), each slightly different. From experience, the hearer would be aware of the repetition of the first three, less aware of the repetition of the second element, and most unlikely to notice any repetition of any total combined sequence, even assuming that anyone listened to it for that length of time.

Thus there would be a continual weaving of the familiar with the novel or unexpected.

It could be set up with concealed speakers in the walls (preferably paired and slightly away from each other to give the sense of the voice not coming from any particular direction) either in a corridor or corner where people passed or lingered occasionally.

The volume would be at a quiet conversational level so that the litany appeared to be coming out of the air, existing in the space, perhaps almost as if whispered into the ear. It would not demand attention, merely offer itself. It would not be expected that anyone would listen for any length of time but just register the flavour of it for perhaps three or four sequences.

Gael Turnbull

The Without Day Fireworks Assortment will be a commemorative boxed set of fireworks, destined to be lit on specific occasions in the future.

Just as in 1707 when the prospect of the reopening of a Scottish Parliament may have been imagined as a distant hope, each firework in the assortment box will be named for a future, longed for, prospect.

The rocket will, of course, be lit at the opening of the New Scottish Parliament. Some other fireworks will be named for achievable goals or occasions within the control of the owner of the box, so as to prevent discouragement, others will be destined for more ambitious occasions.

The box will be modest in size so that many people can afford to buy it. Ideally, a sponsor should be found to supply the boxes as free gifts. Of course some will find it difficult to resist lighting them all at once, so replacements will need to be made available at extra cost. The box would be compartmentalised so that burnt out fireworks could be returned; these would add to the drama of the narrative. Suggested contents of the box, labelled as follows will be:

Rocket	'Without Day'
Two Squibs	'On reaching the top of the first Munro' 'On reaching the top of the last Munro'
Packet of six Sparklers'	'A homecoming'
Jumping Jack	'When equal numbers of men and women are elected to the Scottish Parliament'
Crackpot	'When Birnham Wood shall come to Dunsinane'
Indoor Table Firework[1]	'When England wins the World Cup'
Roman Candle	'When Scotland wins the World Cup'
Banger	'When something happens to the Sutherland Monument'
Golden Rain	'When the peat is cut'
Bengal Light	'On glimpsing a Capercaillie'
Set Piece	'When human rights are recognised across the planet'

---

1   A pill which produces a smouldering worm.

Lesley Kerman

A Proposal: Tenebris Petimus

Walk along a city centre street. Observe the dour buildings, brooding under a sky like an under-exposed photograph. Glance at a passer-by and witness the glower thrown at the smiling stranger. Look to the rugged mass of the Salisbury Crags, setting for The Ettrick Shepherd's masterpiece of Sin and Depravity, looming like judging Elders above the emerging Scottish Parliament. Gaze beyond to the cold glimmer of the Forth as a mean smirr of rain drifts across the November dusk gathering over the city. Our Heritage of darkness and cloud. Our people, happier in shadow and drizzle than in light and sun. Our Parliament, emerging below the ancient volcanic detritus of the crags, reaching into the Millennium and Millennia beyond.

My proposal spans our Past and Future, reaching into the primal bedrock of our psyche, whilst employing a 21st Century interface of micro-electronics, marine biology, psychiatry and ergonomics. I propose the development, manufacture and distribution, via our Public Health Authorities, of the Caledonian Darkness Box. This invention will aid the hundreds and thousands of Scots whose lives are blighted by the depredations of Seasonal Affective Disorder during the Spring and Summer months, tolerating the untold annual Hell of extended daylight hours and increased sunlight. The present author can attest to the effects of Summer Depression the nausea, the dawn sweats, the grinding afternoon headaches triggered by excessive light, the sudden and inescapable urge to flee to a sanctuary of darkness and cold. Panic attacks, sustained periods of convulsions and suicide are not uncommon in severe cases. The box, secretly developed by an anonymous North Uist porpoise flenser, utilises fibre optics, high-performance outboard motor oil and a light-digesting enzyme derived from the secretions of the pineal gland of the Giant Atlantic Squid.

Hitherto, curative therapy has proven either ineffectual or prohibitively expensive. One of the few documented cases of successful treatment featured a group of sufferers who spent the Winter months in Shetland in order to maximise Darkness Absorption and the remainder of the year in Tierra del Fuego. This pattern promoted short-term emotional equilibrium but in the final analysis involved prohibitively expensive travel and subsistence costs. Various strategies initiated by Self-Help organisations involved groups of sufferers enjoying Winter excursions within the Arctic Circle, alternated with periods of Summer residence in the Falkland Islands. Such initiatives, alas, proved only partially successful, and on return to Scotland, subjects drained their reserves of Darkness before the end of Summer. Subsequent remission involved dramatic mood-swings, alcoholism and random violence.

The Darkness Box currently exists as a prototype in the form of a modified herring crate incorporating a front section resembling a flat screen television. The device is placed on any convenient surface and can be used indoors or outside. It is portable and ecologically efficient, powered by the natural light which is negated during operation. A series of points flicker then darken across the screen coalescing into storm-like whorls which dim hypnotically, until the entire screen pulsates with negative light. Swirling masses of blackness sweep across the screen, creating a template upon which the subject can project the darkest of psychic imaginings, discerning within the Rorschach of abstract shapes a favoured rain-swept landscape, a glowering visage or a bleak urban wasteland. The inventor has created a series of relaxation tapes to accompany the device, and it is possible to stare into the darkness of the box on a bright June day while listening to the authentically evoked sounds of storm-driven hail lashing against rattling, ill-fitting window frames. A range of peripherals includes The Dusk Simulator, an enhancement which ensures that the subject always awakes in a slowly-darkening room, and The Ambient Chiller, utilising a photosensitive thermostat which lowers room temperature to match the gathering darkness created by the Simulator.

It is the duty of the Parliament to promote mass-production and delivery to homes throughout the land so that every man, woman and child in Scotland enjoys access to the effects of the Darkness Box, regardless of wealth or status. The benefits of widescreen boxes in public bars, restaurants and pre-school playgroups will be obvious. Giant screens should enrich civic life in cinemas, football grounds and our public parks. Politicians must take steps to ensure that the device occupies a central role in our culture and, to this end, can set no finer example that to arrange immediate installation in Holyrood, commencing every Parliamentary session with prolonged and solemn observance of The Giant Caledonian Darkness Box of the Scottish Parliament.

The server might not exist, it may have existed in the past. Perhaps the server exists already but is as yet undiscovered. Setting ourselves the task of discovering or designing the server's form, location, or function, we have written a series of e-mails sending them to addresses constructed from our notions of what the server might be:

TO: *anyone@The Republic.com*
Do you function as a kind of ideal community, where morality can be achieved in a balance of wisdom, courage and restraint? Is this server a tool for internal life as much as social morality?

TO: *anyone@unknown.com*
We are coming down to London next weekend and wondered if we could meet up for a drink?

TO: *event@collectivememory.com*
Do you know about a series of unrecorded encounters, incidents or experiences which took place within spaces which no longer exist?

TO: *revolution@utopia.com*
Are you based on a model that began with ideas discussed in the writings of Marx and Engels during the mid nineteenth century?

TO: *defined@undefined.com*
Are you a constantly changing set of relationships, defining yourself as that which is not all that you have been defined as?

Ryan Doolan and Bryan Davies

On the Day: A Corrective Ceremony

This project envisages a commemorative, reflective and mnemonic space in the form of a small wood of deciduous and evergreen trees to be planted within the grounds of the new Parliament.

Each new constituency will work out the detail of the processes by which the project is to be realised. Children's involvement from the outset is essential.

1. A tree is chosen to represent each of the seventy-three constituencies; there is a reason given for the choice. Perhaps there will be an open competition in a local newspaper: 'Which tree would you choose to represent our constituency? Give your reason (historical, mythical, heraldic, literary, environmental, spiritual) in no more than twenty words.'

2. A bucket of kelp is collected from the coast of the constituency or, if the constituency has no coastline, from that nearest to it: we are none of us far from the sea in Scotland. Perhaps a local primary school has achieved some remarkable success or a class within one. The kelp is collected as part of a bonus trip to the seaside.

3. The bucket of kelp and the tree are carried in inventive relays to arrive in Edinburgh on the appointed day. Local running clubs and sports clubs use this as an opportunity to raise money for charity.

4. Before (2) and (3) a poetry competition is held among the primary school pupils of each constituency – those for whom the Parliament must act, those who will see growth in the woodland copse by the time they are eligible to vote.

The competition is to complete the following six-line poem:

In this kelp
I plant a tree
Scotland of the land and sea . . .

The completed poem will suggest something of Scotland's future, the vision of its youth, and will be written in any of Scotland's languages.

5. At the planting ceremony, each poem will be recited as its tree is planted. Attached to the tree will be a permanent tag bearing the poem and any relevant details. All children involved in the project will be in attendance as witnesses and thereafter as celebrants.

6. In years to come, MSPs and other government officials will use the wood as a cloister to refresh themselves with the clarity of childhood vision and to reflect upon the passage of time...

7. For in time the copse spreads out over the lower slopes of Arthur's Seat – a wild wood where the Capercaillie calls and a wise old wolf patrols; its taste for hypocrisy, hubris and cant indirectly leading to the odd by-election.

Tom Pow

A Proposal for a Public Holiday: 'Beuys Day'

On the anniversary of Joseph Beuys' birthday a single female wolf will be chosen from amongst a pack which has been released on Rannoch Moor. The wolf is secured in a cage and brought to Edinburgh. The floor of the cage is made from a blackboard covered with bracken and moorland grasses. On the morning of 'Beuys Day', at precisely 11 a.m., the wolf is delivered to the Scottish Parliament. The cage is placed in the centre of the debating chamber. Every MSP is present. The Queen and the Prime Minister of Great Britain are present; between them sits an empty chair, upon which Beuys hat is placed. The director of the Scottish Arts Council stands behind this chair in an attitude of solemn contemplation. Jimmy Boyle is in the public gallery. Following a single note sounded on the Caprington Horn Richard Demarco steps forward; with a gleam in his eye he utters a single word *"Joseph"*, and the wolf is released.

A Proposal for a Hot Air Balloon

It is estimated how much breath would have been expended since the final sitting in 1707 to the reinstallment of the new Scottish Parliament in 1999.

(This is based on as accurate estimate as possible, taking into account every factor that might have increased or decreased the amount of breath that could have been expended between these two moments in time).

This quantity of breath, air, is pumped into a balloon, and the balloon in moored above the new Parliament building.

The balloon is lowered and the First Minister pricks the balloon with a silver needle.

Emerge

There is a silly story of a subterranean passage between the Castle and
Holyrood, and a bold Highland piper who volunteered to explore its windings.
He made his entrance by the upper end, playing a strathspey; the curious footed
it after him down the street, following his descent by the sound of the chanter
from below; until all of a sudden, about the level of St Giles's, the music came
abruptly to an end, and the people in the street stood at fault with their hands
uplifted. Whether he was choked with gases, or perished in a quag, or was
removed bodily by the Evil One, remains a point of doubt; but the piper has
never again been seen or heard of from that day to this. Perhaps he wandered
down into the land of Thomas the Rhymer, and some day, when it is least
expected, may take a thought to revisit the sunlit upper world. That will be a
strange moment for the cabmen on the stance beside St Giles's, when they hear
the drone of his pipes reascending from the bowels of the earth below their
horses' feet. Robert Louis Stevenson, *Edinburgh: Picturesque Notes* (1878)

Some time after the establishment of the Holyrood Parliament, the piper
emerges within its precincts, blinking, confused and silent. Steadying
himself, he puffs up his pipes, and blows an old, familiar tune. Buoyed up
by this, he conceives a new theme upon which he plays a series of ever more
dazzling improvisations. Perceiving a nearby building which resembles an
upturned boat, with an effort of the will he rights it, climbs aboard and rides
on the wind towards the open sea, developing his variations as he does so.

A golden cross, or perhaps a star, appears momentarily in the shifting
clouds above Arthur's Seat. Later the vessel is found wrecked off the west
coast of Scotland. The piper himself becomes untraceable.

A claim concerning the missing building is defended by the insurers and
a court case ensues, as part of which the insurers attempt to sue the architect
for negligence.

Competitions:

There are a number of competitions in which you can take part.
The competition categories are:

Music: (a) Suggestions are invited as to an existing pipe-tune which the
piper might play on first emerging; (b) a new theme to complement
this, and to form the basis of an extended improvisation, is also sought.

Nomenclature: A name is sought for the piper's sailing vessel.

Theology: Interpretations of the golden cross, or star, are invited.
Reference may be made to the schismatic traditions of the reformed
Scottish church, and/or to recent ecumenical developments.

Prizes:

The prizes in each category are:

Music: The winning tunes will be recorded, and subsequently broadcast
through specially installed speakers located beneath floor-grilles
throughout the Parliament, randomly as regards location, timing and
volume.

Nomenclature: The winner will be presented with a spar from the wreck
of the sailing vessel, inscribed with the chosen name. A second spar will
be similarly inscribed, and displayed within the Parliament.

Theology: The winner will, in the opinion of the judges which is final,
obtain the grace of God.

Ken Cockburn

As Scotland celebrates having its own legislature for the first time in nearly three hundred years, we might also throw a backward glance at the beginnings of law-making here. Our earliest surviving legal text comes from Iona, promulgated in 697 A.D. by Adomnán, the monastery's abbot. Medieval writers called it *Cáin Adomnáin* in recognition of its author, and *Lex Innocentium*, "the Law of the Innocents", in recognition of its purpose. For Adomnán's law gave protection to folk who, in a society governed by war-lords, could not defend themselves. The "innocents" were those who did not bear arms: women, in the first place, and then children and clergy. So in the eighth century Adomnán was remembered thus:

> *To Adomnán of Iona*
> *whose troop is radiant,*
> *noble Jesus has granted*
> *the lasting freedom of the women of the Gaels.* [1]

As head of a monastery, a community of unarmed men, Adomnán could not impose his Law by force. Instead he struggled to build a consensus that women should be protected from violence. He exploited family connections, the reputation for holiness of his patron and predecessor, Columcille, his own personal prestige as head of a family of monasteries, and his diplomatic and literary skills. According to a tenth century version of the Law text, he also exploited his bell. 'The Bell of Adomnán's Anger', the kind of hand-bell which was standard equipment for senior clergy in medieval Scotland, had its own power. Some kings withstood Adomnán, refusing to protect women in their territories, and Adomnán cursed them, ringing his bell against them:

O humble, gentle lad,
O son armed with the Rule,
strike the bell against Cellach of Carman
that he be in the earth before the year's end . . .

The bell of truly miraculous Adomnán
has laid waste many kings.
Each one against whom it gives battle one thing awaits:
it has laid them waste.

The Bell is therefore a sign of moral authority where the physical power of coercion is lacking. When it is rung, it is rung by the powerless because their rights are violated by the powerful. It is rung by those who believe that the first task of law, and therefore legislators, is to protect the vulnerable and defenceless.

Of course, laws can often express and reinforce patterns of inequality and injustice, leaping to the defence of the already powerful, suppressing the cry of the poor or the weak. But the ringing of Adomnán's Bell should remind legislators, voters, judges, taxation officials, ordinary people – all of us – that the first reason that laws were needed was to protect those without recourse to arms from those who were well armed.

I have heard Adomnán's bell (or at least a replica of it) being rung recently by peace campers at Faslane, protesting against Trident whose weapons are aimed at whole populations of unarmed people, men, women and children. I have heard it rung by the victims of appalling domestic violence now living in a women's refuge. I have heard it rung by refugees and by victims of sexual abuse. I have heard it rung by ordinary men and women who swung these five and a half kilograms of worked iron, not very musically, because their hearts rose up against more kinds of oppression than I can number.

Adomnán's Bell should be a permanent clanking reminder to us all of what law is for. I would like the nation to appoint a Dewar, a guardian of the Bell. This person would be independent of all political parties, all sections of society, but the job would be a god-like one: to 'hear the cry of the poor' (*Psalm 34)* and to ring the Bell in protest, to raise an outcry wherever oppression was taking place. The Dewar would be a national figure, honoured in Parliament and Court, not as a debater of policy or strategy, but as a prophetic figure. The Bell and its Dewar would appear at picket-lines, at warrant sales, at submarine bases, outside prisons, at demonstrations – a disturbing and unpredictable figure, perhaps sometimes like a fool, but a holy fool. Sometimes like a prophet, sometimes like a performer in street theatre, ringing the Bell, and inviting others to ring it, as an outcry against the misuse of power against the powerless, as a reminder of the meaning of law.

1   Whitley Stokes, *The Martyrology of Oengus the Culdee* (London, 1905), 196.

A Proposal for a New Scottish Parliament

FREE THE MASONS

Pavel Büchler

Reachdan Ur/Sean: An Old/New Constitution

I decided to scrap my original project a (satirical) ceremony akin to the rites of oriental ancestor-worship in which contemporary MSPs apologise (in Gàidhlig) to countless Scots damaged or neutralised or extinguished due to the political climate over the last three centuries. Instead, more positively, I have opted to provide a translation of P. A. Payutto's *A Constitution for Living: Buddhist Principles For a Fruitful and Harmonious Life.* Payutto (recipient of a UNESCO Prize for Peace Education) has written a handbook for life which is of untellable benefit to Buddhists and non-Buddhists alike. Whether focusing on political participation or on everyday household life, his advice is simple but penetrating, attentive but enlightening.

Compassion rather than cynicism? Harmony rather than conflict? Surely these 2500 year old teachings are too radical?

In this excerpt I envisage a bilingual Pali/Gàidhlig chant to be sung at the opening of Parliament:

Jarādhammatā tha a h-uile duin' againn a' fàs nas aosda.

(We are all, all of us, growing older.)

Byādhidhammatā tha a h-uile duin' againn buailteach air a bhith tinn aig àm sam bith.

(We are all, all of us, prone to sickness at any time.)

Maranadhammatā bàsachaidh sinn uile, uaireigin.

(We shall, all of us, at some time, die.)

Piyavinābhāvatā thèid dealachadh a chur eadar a h-uile duin' againn agus na rudan air a bheil gaol againn.

(*We shall, all of us, be separated from that which we love.*)

Kammassakatā a h-uile rud a nà sinn – math neo dona – bidh buaidh aige oirnn-fhin uaireigin san àm ri teachd.

(*Everything we do, good or bad, shall bear upon us sometime in the future.*)

A Proposal for A Compendium

If the re-examination of cultural icons is required, as I think it is, to ensure Scotland's visionary future; then I propose a series of satirical interventions which will focus our view on major characters which have moulded society.

A symbolic presence is needed to supercharge the spirit of this new Scottish Parliament and its site at Holyrood. Admittedly there could and should be hundreds of international cultural sources to energise the parliament and the people of Scotland; but I have chosen three initially to illustrate the idea. As they died in relative obscurity with more than a degree of drama, I felt that a phoenix-like renaissance was appropriate.

If symbols or reliquaries relating to each icon were placed in the fabric and foundations of the building; what would they be and where would they be located. I might propose that

The 'bones' of Thomas Paine could be set at the threshold of the main debating chamber. (In a glass covered box on the floor.)

The 'spectacles' of Patrick Geddes would be given in turn to each speaker to improve their 'vision'!

A replica of the pistol which Hugh Miller shot himself with could be presented to MSPs who commit a misdemeanour – or are not re-elected! (As the equivalent of a golden handshake!)

I would propose modifying a copy of the site plans to include a generous list of cultural icons and symbols with which we might associate. I would encourage participation from the reader who would be asked to make their own judgement of which icons should be included in the building and how this might ensure the successful running of the parliament. If the reader felt bold enough they could write their own remarks on the enclosed copy of the plan. Or they could make a few photocopies – and experiment!

A New Sense of Paine

'Our style and manner of thinking have undergone a revolution'

The exhumed bones of Thomas Paine were transported to England in 1819 and lost in Liverpool or London.

Patrick Passes On

'By Leaves we Live'

In 1932 Sir Patrick Geddes died and was taken from Montpellier to Marseilles for cremation. His wife witnessed his hair and beard exploding into flames.

Miller Moves

'Pterichthys Milleri'

Hugh Miller shot himself in 1856 and was buried at the Grange, Edinburgh.

It is no accident that *Brigadoon* is set in Scotland. Or – more precisely – the image of *Brigadoon* is located in Scotland, although actually manufactured elsewhere. (Producer Arthur Freed notoriously *"went to Scotland but . . . could find nothing that looked like Scotland."*) To the world at large Scotland is (perceived as) a place that exists outwith time.

This timeless image, or image of timelessness, has, of course a history of its own. When, in 1707, Scotland's Parliament was adjourned, this represented a collective decision by the Scottish nation to step outside the course of historical development. A new entity – Great Britain – became the vehicle of historical progress, and the great thinkers of the Scottish Enlightenment turned their minds to explaining this vehicle – how it was constructed and where it was going. Scotland for its part became a nation with a glorious Scottish past and a glorious British future.

Brigadoon has no place in this disenchanted world of engineers, missionaries and bureaucrats it belongs in the realm of the Celtic twilight, of noble savages preserved (in aspic) from the ravages of progress. The native Scottish sources of this image are obvious enough, in 'Ossian' MacPherson and Walter Scott. For them, the Gaels are glorious doomed warriors, immortal in song and impotent in life, unable to reproduce either sexually or culturally. And, largely through the work of Scott, these archetypal Gaels became the symbols of Scotland as a whole, progenitors or the tartan kailyard. Scott's art was to conceal the psychic tensions between the historiography of progress and the politics of reaction. Throughout the 19th century and into the 20th, the compromise he brokered allowed Scots to have their bannock and eat it too; they could enjoy the fruits of the empire without either sacrificing their mythic past or letting any disruptive political genies out of the bottle. Under the long hegemony of ethical liberalism, Scottish politics took on an other-worldly air, debating how best to construct the godly commonwealth of Knox and Chalmers in an unregenerate world. Since (everyone knew) none of these plans would ever negotiate the rapids of Westmister, politics entered the realm of make-believe (Peter Pan as a Scottish archetype.)

Materially this state of suspended animation did Scotland no harm. Individually, many Scots did well out of the empire being psychologically thirled to a progressive British Whig ideology was probably a positive economic advantage. The counterbalancing costs kicked in on the cultural, moral and spiritual side. As individuals, Scots might be held responsible for their actions (Calvinism is very hot on individual responsibility). But as a group the Scots were precluded from any kind of political inter-vention, and as a result they lapsed into a kind of detached *accidie*.

In this light, the establishment of the new Parliament opens up an opportunity for Scotland to re-enter political time, restarting the clock that stopped in 1707, and to resume collective responsibility for its own future. The *Brigadoon* complex can be deconstructed. One step would be to create a virile post-Ossian Gaelic culture asserting its own vision in the face of the world – an aghaidh nan creag. Another would be to recognise the real complexities and ambiguities of Scotland – ethnic, linguistic, geographical, etc. – against the facile stereotypes.

So what's the project? To make a sequel to *Brigadoon* – one manufactured in Scotland, in which the spell in broken and at a bound, local heroes are free to re-enter the 'real' world. Think of the options – script by Irvine Welsh? Soundtrack by Martyn Bennett? Settings by Andy Goldworthy? Costumes by Alexander MacQueen? Choreography by Craig Brown? The possibilities are boundless. Auditions on 6 May 1999.

Dennis Smith

A Proposal Fur a Wee Faisalabad Haggis Kebab Caery-Oot

Ah propose tae set up an 'abad in the middlae the Glesgae Shields (commonly known as Wee Faisalabad).

This will take the form ae a theme park, consistin ae several dry cooshite dwellins an a big duff, the size ae a tenement frae which will be dispensed two-foot seech kebabs (not sheikh, shish or Sikh) made ae halaal haggis, thegither wi giant tartan tumblers ae Irn Bru.

Specifically referrin tae the Haggis Kebab outlet, Ah propose that it will be womanned by six wee Faisalabadis (colloquially sometimes referred tae as The Shields Girls) who will be dressed in tartan kamises and kilts made fae fine Punjabi silk. The workers will smile constantly, and will be called by their first names and will be paid the lowest possible Euro-rate in Secus (Scottish Ecus).

The only music allowed will be:

Flower ae Scotland *which will be played in binary form on duff drums*

Christian singin Yabba-dabba-doo (*the original version*)

The Punjabi rock group, Vital Signs intoning Long Live Pakistan, Land Of The Pure!

Prices will vary in relation tae the kisaan calendar, and also wi the time ae day, the direction ae the wind etc. The sign above the windae will read 1707 OR BUST! The number ae kebabs to be cooked weekly must always total, seventeen-hundred-an-seven. Opening nicht will be 6 May 1999, at precisely wan meenut past midnight, Shields-time.

Fae the mud ae Faisalabad
Will I mould the bones ae Glasgee

In the steamin hot Bhangra nights ae east Punjab
The Cailleach dances her frozen dance
While the street-corner Gangsta declaims
That life has always been like this

The People of the Opium

At the front door of Parliament House, a flower bed. Its centre shows the Scottish flag – the blue in Scottish bluebells, plastic, made in Hong Kong, the saltire picked out in bits of silver cash. This is the flag that flew on the ships of Dr. Jardine and Mr. Mathieson when they peddled opium in the Pearl River Estuary. Let there be a silver skull in the top quarter of the saltire.

Silver was the only commodity the Chinese wanted from the West, so when supply ran short, a new need was created for them. A patch of Remembrance Day poppies at the bottom right corner of the flower bed represents Hong Kong island.

In the 1830s the opium trade was going so well that Jardine and Mathieson were taking on all the tonnage they could. A model of the Psyche, bottom left, sailing towards Hong Kong: it was converted from a slaver on the Atlantic run to an opium clipper in the South China Sea.

When he retired to Scotland, Mathieson bought the Isle of Lewis. Not long after that, its inhabitants were threatened with famine by the potato blight. Mathieson fed the islanders, and that earned him a baronetcy. A patch of potatoes top left represents Lewis. This may also remind MSPs of the Tory parliamentarian who suggested that Hong Kong residents with right of abode who wished to migrate to the United Kingdom in 1997 be sent to a Scottish island.

Top right, a black marble stele inscribed with the letter from Governor Lin of Canton to Queen Victoria. The inscription is in Chinese characters, in the Governor's calligraphy. There is no need for an English translation since (a) the messsage did not get through, or was not acted upon, and (b) every Scot will know it better than the Declaration of Arbroath:

Let us ask, where is your conscience? I have heard that the smoking of opium is very strictly forbidden in your country; that is because the harm caused by opium is clearly understood. Since it is not permitted to do harm to your own country, then even less should you let such harm be passed on to other countries – especially China! Of all that China exports to foreign countries, there is not a single thing which is not of benefit when resold; all are beneficial. Is there a single article from China which has done any harm to foreign countries? Take tea and rhubarb, for example; the foreign countries cannot get along for a single day without them. If China cuts off these benefits with no sympathy for those who are to suffer, then what can the barbarians rely upon to keep themselves alive?

Behind the flower bed stands a very large billboard. The message on the hoarding will of course change from time to time, but the first might appear as follows: an image of Monument Valley, Arizona; on the valley floor, tens of thousands of coolies are smoking hookahs or cigarettes. The legend reads:

WARNING: WELCOME TO THE BIG COUNTRY

A Proposal for a Public Holiday: Dolly Mixture Day

It will be a decision unforeseen in the Scotland Act: the cloning of the Scottish people, led by the First Minister. The Scottish people will lay the foundations of a species both asexual and immortal, putting an end to individuality, selfishness, national egoism, and the sex-death nexus at the heart of our fallen civilisation.

On 'Dolly Mixture Day', the city of Edinburgh will come to an almost complete standstill. From the Roslin Institute will be transported by gun carriage Dolly the Sheep, accompanied by a platoon of soldiers from the King's Own Scottish Borderers. The procession will penetrate the Pubic Triangle of Tollcross, then bid farewells to the statue of David Hume and the Fleshmarket Close. A respectful salute will be given in the direction of John Knox's House.

The gun-carriage will halt at the Holyrood Parliament. It will be there that the sacrifice of Dolly will take place. Every great civilisation is founded on murder and Dolly will go to her fate with dignity, emitting one last happy bleat to the solemn gathering. She will be beheaded by Mary Stuart's axe as she lies trembling on the Stone of Destiny. Then the Butcher Laureate will proceed to cut her up, not into gigot, but rather into kebabs that will be distributed to Iraqi orphans, in a gesture of atonement.

As the odour of grilled meat rises into the Nation's sky, there will be released on Arthur's Seat a flock of cloned sheep, happy to munch any Nation's grass. A flypast from R.A.F Lossiemouth will salute the new and beautiful sterility.

At this moment, the First Minister will shoot one last hypocritical look to his soon-to-be-obsolete family and hand himself over to the soldiers of the gun-carriage, which duly will transport him to the Roslin Institute. Five million souls will follow him.

That day, sweetshops will be open and unattended by adults, with large jars of Dolly Mixtures within reach of children. Market relations will be discarded, and the children will eat till they vomit from their individual greed. On each cash-till will stand a bust of John Knox.

The message of a new civilisation will be broadcast to the world from upturned boats, whose hulls will at last give a place in the sun to barnacles and wrack. And thus the sun will set on the fallen past, like the last bubbles struggling up to the tangy waves.

A Proposal for a New Scottish Parliament

The Parliament Building under construction in Holyrood will be at least the third existent Edinburgh location in which the Scottish Parliament has sat.

One is the scrapped version lying redundant on Calton Hill. With some due attention it could be operational, but is deemed too dated in appearance to accurately represent the new interior machinations.

Another is the Assembly Halls hired from the Church of Scotland. It is higher than the other two and points skyward, implying a lengthier journey is possible than the one the temporary controllers have in mind.

The next building is a Spanish designed, purpose built model. The external appearance is intended to reflect the forward thinking ideas being developed on the inside. The interior will be user friendly, comfortable and modern.

Naturally, the newest vehicle will house many different occupants over the years. At any given point there must also be a keeper, someone responsible for the journey being undertaken by the party, advising what route to follow and which direction to take. This keeper must also avail himself to the public in a way they recognise and understand, revealing his identity, that of his party and of any changes within or to the fabric of the Scottish Parliament Building.

The form opposite should be completed by every new keeper and will then be available from all Post Offices in Scotland.

Stuart Bennett

SCOTTISH PARLIAMENT REGISTRATION DOCUMENT

PLEASE WRITE IN BLACK INK AND CAPITAL LETTERS

KEEPER DETAILS – *if any details in section A change, please write new details in section B*

A   Registered Keeper – Please note the registered keeper is not necessarily the Parliament's legal owner

....

Registration Mark ....

The previous recorded keeper is: ....

B   Mr ☐   Mrs ☐   Miss ☐   *Please tick the relevant box*

Title or business name ....

Forenames in full ....

Surname ....

Address ....

Post Town ....

Postcode .... *Please help us to help you by using your postcode*

If the keeper has changed, tick box and give the date of sale or transfer ☐   ...... / ...... / ......

New keeper's politician licence number ....

PARLIAMENT DETAILS – *if any details in section D change, please write new details in section E*

C   Present age (to last completed year) ....

Scrapped ☐   Exported ☐   *please tick*   Date of Scrapping/Export ...... / ...... / ......

D   Make .... Model/Type .... Date of Registration ...... / ...... / ......

Last change of Keeper ...... / ...... / ......   No. of Former Keepers

Revenue .... Weight .... Colour .... Seating Capacity...........

Taxation Class ....

E   CHANGES OF PARLIAMENT DETAILS – *please enter new details*

Body Type .... New Revenue Weight ....Date of Change ...... / ...... / ......

New Colour .... Seating Capacity...................Taxation Class ....

DECLARATION

Registered Keeper (to sign in all cases) – *I declare that the new details I have given are true to the best of my knowledge.*

Registered Keeper... Date ....

New Keeper (if applicable) – *I declare that this parliament was sold or transferred to me on the date shown in section B above and my name and address are correct.*

New Keeper ....Date ....

A Proposal for the Debating Chamber of a New Scottish Parliament: Cerulean Blue

Within a radiation proof enclosed inspection chamber made of glass with glove inlets, sited in the cellar below the Debating Chamber a one inch cube of building fabric from the core of Dounreay Nuclear Power Station is to be placed. This will be continually layered with coats of lead paint until its radioactive charge is sealed, and will be safe to show outside of its protective casing in the Debating Chamber directly above the position it was worked on.

Ian Balch

A Proposal: The Hall of Unsung Heroes and Heroines

The new Scottish Parliament building will have a Hall of Unsung Heroes/ Heroines in which will be displayed, on plinths, pedestals and in alcoves, marble and bronze busts of Scottish people of whom nobody but their immediate families has ever heard.

A Proposal for Without Day
The following inscription, cut in Scotch Roman on a slab of Iona marble:

SINE DIE
SYNE DEE

Hamish Whyte

A Proposal

A. Locations Speak

Stornoway Stromness Inverness Aberdeen Glasgow Dundee Edinburgh Hamilton
6th May 1999

Recordings made out on the streets on the day of the Scottish Election: people stopped at random in various parts of Scotland and asked fourteen questions:

B. Ways of Asking
1. Why are you in this particular place today?
2. Can you describe what you can see in the particular place we are standing in?
3. Where have you come from?
4. Where are you going?
5. What is important about today?
6. What do you expect from the new Scottish Parliament?
7. How do you think it will change your life?
8. What do you hope for once the Parliament has been established?
9. What needs to be changed in Scotland?
10. What are the good things that should stay the same?
11. How important is Edinburgh to you?
12. Name five places that are important to you.
13. Name five people who are important to you.
14. In a word, what is the atmosphere in Scotland today?

C. Ways of Saying

Layers of the voice communicate – the texture of memory, of history, of experience, of the present, of the past, of the future, of aspiration, of resignation, of gender, of age, of weather, of time, of regret, of nostalgia, of optimism, or pessimism, of received 'spin', of community, of isolation, of closeness, of identity, of displacement, of humour, of vulnerability, of confidence, of a lack of confidence, of pride, of suspicion, of self consciousness, of power, of identity, of a loss of identity, of creating identity.

D. Ways of Hearing

The work constructs a pattern of articulation, not a narrative – a network of clues, of innuendo, of the seen, the unseen, of the said, of the unsaid. Information that only the voice can provide – of the desire to be heard – to say – non history makers or history writers become history makers, history speakers, and the central source of history – a history of the present – a present not a history – those that live it and experience it. No filters, no shortcuts, no secondary accounts only the primary, only knowledge, memory, the present, the past, the future.

The impossibility of memorialising – only the possibility of reflection of the now.

The work is initiated/completed/by the listener/audience/participant.

William Furlong

Memo

My apologies
I missed your deadline.
It turned out to be more difficult than I expected
making a non-existent artwork in text. I had ideas
but they all seemed so enticing as I fell asleep at night
yet so impossible when I faced the computer next morning.

What I first had in mind was
taking out the floors in the Members' building
and replacing them with glass.
A sort of observation hive
where looking up or down
would be to see the repetition of ones own activity.
Forcing a sense of fragility rather than power
of participation over importance.

But it all seemed too moral.
What I really wanted was an idea
singular, ironic, witty
clever. All summed
up in a dazzling sentence of Haiku like
simplicity
a showpiece in fact.

Then the penny dropped
art/politics
human nature
dreams lost to reality
its all the same.

Perhaps
resolution if there is one
does lie
after all
in transparency.

Su Grierson

A Proposal

A Proposal

A Proposal

A Proposal

Index of Authors

pocketbooks

Summer 1998

01   GREEN WATERS
      An anthology of boats and voyages, edited by Alec Finlay;
      featuring poetry, prose and visual art by Ian Stephen,
      Ian Hamilton Finlay, Graham Rich.
      ISBN 0 9527669 2 2; paperback, 96pp, colour illustrations, reprinting.

Spring 2000

02   ATOMS OF DELIGHT
      An anthology of Scottish haiku and short poems, edited with an
      Introduction by Alec Finlay, and a Foreword by Kenneth White.
      ISBN 0 7486 6275 8; paperback, 208pp, £7.99.

03   LOVE FOR LOVE
      An anthology of love poems, edited by John Burnside and
      Alec Finlay, with an Introduction by John Burnside.
      ISBN 0 7486 6276 6; paperback, 200pp, £7.99.

04   WITHOUT DAY
      An anthology of proposals for a new Scottish Parliament, edited
      by Alec Finlay, with an introduction by David Hopkins. *Without
      Day* includes an Aeolus CD by William Furlong.
      ISBN 0 7486 6277 4; paperback with CD, 184pp, £7.99 (including VAT).

Autumn 2000

05   WISH I WAS HERE
        A multicultural, multilingual poetry anthology, edited by
        Kevin MacNeil and Alec Finlay, with an Aeolus CD.

06   WILD LIFE
        Hamish Fulton, walking artist, works made in the Cairngorms.
        Wild Life includes an Aeolus CD.

07   A DAY BOOK
        David Shrigley

Available through all good bookshops.

Book trade orders to:
Scottish Book Source, 137 Dundee Street, Edinburgh EH11 1BG.

Copies are also available from:
Morning Star Publications, Canongate Venture (5), New Street,
Edinburgh EH8 8BH.

Website: www.pbks.co.uk

Without Day

An Aeolus CD by William Furlong

Recorded May 6th, 1999 on location by:

Glasgow	David Bellingham
Stornoway	Ian Stephen
Stromness	Ruth Fraser
Inverness	Gary Maclean
Aberdeen	Zoë Irvine
Dundee	Zoë Irvine
Edinburgh	Stuart MacFarlane
Hamilton	Students of Bell College

Edited by William Furlong
Additional editing by Zoë Irvine

Produced by Zoë Irvine
Mastered at Aeolus, 2000

aeolus_sound @yahoo.com
Tel: (44) 7775 740 969

With thanks to Alec Finlay, Moray Firth Radio, Ronnie Bergman at
Bell College and all those who helped with the recordings.